The C O L O R

of

J O Y

By

Julianne MacLean

ISBN: 1927675243
ISBN 13: 9781927675243

Prologue

Riley James

It pains me to admit this, but there was a time in my life when I believed happiness was an illusion, or at the very least, a concept spitefully invented to make us all feel inadequate when we failed to achieve it.

In my youth, I was the quintessential angry young man. I was wild and brooding, and the harder my father tried to whip me into shape and create a future leader out of me, the deeper I fell into the dark and dangerous world of rebellion.

Although "fell" isn't quite the right word. What I did was cannonball off the high diving board to create as big a splash as possible. I wanted to drown my father in the tidal wave of my anger and resentment. Become the exact opposite of what he wanted me to be. Show him that his strict disciplinarian tactics had failed. I did an excellent job of it, too.

They say youth is wasted on the young. I'm not sure if that's true, but I do know that I did not experience joy until much later in life, after I hit rock bottom in my late teens and early twenties. This terrible fall from grace included two brief prison incarcerations and substance abuse problems that are thankfully behind me now.

I'm proud to say I'm a new man. Perhaps not quite the man my father wanted me to be. I'm not a brain surgeon, a lawyer or a politician, but at least I know what love is. Love and respect for myself and others, and that is where I believe true joy is found.

I wish we could always be in control of our destinies in this quest for joy in life, but sometimes the earth collapses under our feet and a sinkhole opens up. What can we do but drop and hope for the best? Or at least hope for an eventual understanding of why this terrible thing happened.

Perhaps the lesson is this: Without knowledge of misery, there can be no true knowledge of joy.

Riley

November 12

S ure. Life is full of ups and downs, but we all know that some downs are worse than others. There are those from which we simply cannot recover. Or at least it might seem that way when we're in the depths of the worst possible scenario.

"I don't know how much longer I can take this," Lois said, breathing through another contraction. "What's she waiting for?"

"The perfect moment, I guess." After twenty-two hours of labor, it was a dedicated attempt to lighten the tension and diminish my fears.

It all began at home the previous day when we sat down at the kitchen table for dinner. Lois's mother Carol, who'd arrived a week earlier to help out with our two young children, had cooked a giant pot of Chicken Fiesta Soup. At first I thought it was too spicy for Lois because as soon as she tasted it, she dropped her spoon on the floor.

"You don't like it?" Carol asked.

"It's not that." Lois rose heavily from her chair and looked down at the floor. "I think my water just broke."

The kids looked down as well. "Did you pee your pants, Mummy?"

Carol ran around the table to assess the situation.

An hour later, Lois and I were checked into the obstetrics unit at the hospital.

⸻

"I feel more relaxed this time," she said, rubbing a hand over her swollen belly as she climbed onto the bed.

"They say third time's a charm," I replied. "Though the first two were pretty great."

Both our children had been born on their exact due dates after only a few hours of labor. Danny was now six years old and Trudy was four. They were smart as whips and got along well with each other.

"I just wish we could decide on the name," Lois said. "I like both of them."

We already knew we were having a girl and we'd narrowed it down to two names: Jordan or Morgan.

"We'll know as soon as we see her," I suggested, sitting forward in my chair to rest my elbows on my knees. "We don't need to decide until then."

Lois nodded and focused on her toes. "There's another contraction coming. How long has it been?"

I checked my watch. "About eight minutes since the last one."

She panted in a staccato rhythm until it was over, then sat back and relaxed again. "I can't wait to see her," she said with a smile. "It's going to be so great to get her home. Trudy will be so excited."

I squeezed Lois's hand.

⸻

Twenty-one hours later, we were still waiting for Lois's cervix to fully dilate. It was now 5:00 p.m. the following day and neither of us had slept a wink through the steady labor pains happening every five minutes. We were both exhausted and growing increasingly discouraged because we knew it couldn't go on much longer. The doctor had explained that she'd have to perform a C-section if the baby wasn't delivered within twenty-four hours after Lois's water broke. Lois was still keen to deliver the baby the old-fashioned way, so she was holding out.

Another labor pain began and Lois breathed through it with a tight jaw and a face drenched in perspiration. As soon as it was over, she lay back and stared up at the ceiling. "Can you get the nurse?" she asked. "I want her to check me again to see if I'm dilated more, because if I'm not, I'm ready to give in. I'm so tired, Riley. I don't think I can push this baby out anyway."

I stood quickly and went out into the hall where I found Brenda, the obstetrical nurse who had come on duty a few hours earlier. She was talking to the young medical student who had been observing our case all day.

"Hey," I said, "Lois is at the end of her rope. Can you check her again?"

"Of course." Brenda followed me back to our room with the student, pulled on a pair of gloves and examined my wife. "Still only six centimeters," she said with a note of apology. "This little one just doesn't want to come out."

"She'll be a handful," Lois said, looking up at me with a pained expression. "Strong-willed. Digging her heels in."

Wishing I was better at hiding my unease, I simply nodded.

Lois let out a deep breath. "I guess I'm just going to have to surrender to the idea of a C-section. It's not the end of the world.

It'll just take longer to recover. I'm sure Mom will be happy to stay an extra week if we need her to."

Just then, Lois winced and sat up. "Ow! Something hurts!" She clutched her right side.

Brenda removed her gloves, dropped them into the garbage pail and moved around the bed to check the monitor. "Does it feel like a contraction?" she asked.

Lois shook her head. "No, it's different, like something is ripping me apart. Oh, God, here comes another contraction."

She breathed through it until it passed, then flopped back onto the pillows, grimaced and shut her eyes.

Brenda pressed a button on the monitor to print out a tape.

"There were a few early decelerations after the last couple of contractions," she said as she looked at it, "but otherwise the tracing looks pretty good. The baby's heart rate is normal in between."

Brenda invited the medical student closer to watch the next contraction on the monitor, but when it began, it wouldn't stop. Lois breathed through it as long as she could, then she cried out in agony. "What's happening? Why won't the pain go away?"

Brenda felt Lois's belly for a brief moment, then spoke quietly to the medical student. "Go get Dr. Orlean. Tell her there's no deceleration in the contractions and we might be looking at an abruption or a possible uterine rupture."

I didn't know what any of that meant, but the word rupture didn't sound good. A burning heat filled my stomach.

Lois was writhing in pain on the bed. I tried to hold her hand but she slapped me away and clutched her stomach.

"Turn over onto your left side," Brenda ordered in a firm voice as she scrambled to put Lois on oxygen.

Dr. Orlean ran into the room. I was never so glad to see a doctor in my entire life.

"Something's wrong," I said to her. "She's in really bad pain."

"Please step back."

Helpless and panicked, I moved to the far wall while the doctor checked the tape from the monitor.

"Get an ultrasound in here," she said. "*Stat!*"

Brenda ran out while the medical student watched with wide eyes—as if she had no more idea than I did what would happen next.

"Can you tell me exactly where the pain is?" Dr. Orlean asked Lois.

She pointed to her side and ground out words through clenched teeth. "It's right here, and it hurts like hell."

Brenda ran back into the room pushing a portable ultrasound machine on wheels. The doctor raised Lois's gown, quickly squirted gel on her belly, and ran the probe over the area.

"There's no rupture," she said as she focused on the screen image, "but oh…look here…"

I strode forward. "What is it?"

The medical student came closer as well.

"There's a separation of the placenta." Dr. Orlean continued to slide the probe over Lois's belly, searching for something. "And there's the clot."

"Heart rate's still eighty," Brenda said.

"It's definitely an abruption." Dr. Orlean set down the probe and leaned over Lois. "Mrs. James, we're going to take you to the OR and do a section right away." She exchanged a look with Brenda, who called for more help to get Lois moved onto a stretcher.

"What's an abruption?" I asked the med student.

"It's where part of the placenta separates from the uterus wall prematurely. It causes bleeding. That's the reason for the clot the doctor was talking about. She has to deal with it quickly to make sure the baby's blood supply doesn't get cut off."

"So this is really dangerous?" I replied, barely able to believe any of this was happening as I watched the nurses and orderlies quickly transfer Lois to the stretcher.

The student nodded. "Yes."

I followed them out, running alongside the stretcher as they wheeled Lois down the corridor. "Everything's going to be fine," I said to her, though I had no idea if that were true or not. "I'll be right here with you. I won't leave your side."

"I'm sorry, Mr. James," Brenda said. "There's no time. You'll have to wait outside."

"*Please!*" Lois cried. She grabbed hold of my hand and squeezed it, then writhed in agony.

Brenda spoke to the medical student running behind me. "Can you take care of him? Get him prepped and bring him in?"

"I will," she replied.

I was then forced to let go of Lois's hand as they pushed through a set of double doors and turned left down another corridor. The doors swung shut in front of my face.

My stomach careened. *My wife…My beautiful wife…Please, God, let her be okay.*

I remembered suddenly that we hadn't given a name to the baby yet. I wished now that we had, but everything had spun out of control so quickly. I'd barely had a chance to register it.

The med student touched my shoulder and I turned to her in a numb haze of disbelief. Her words seemed almost garbled as they reached my ears.

"Let's get you in there," she said. "Follow me." She led me into a change room and handed me OR greens, booties and a cap. I felt stunned and baffled.

"Put these on and I'll meet you right outside that door."

"Thank you." I moved to get changed.

By the time we made it to the OR, Lois had just been put under general anesthetic because there was no time for a spinal. The obstetrician was about to cut into her belly.

The med student—I later learned her name was Elaine—led me to a spot by Lois's head where I could stand out of the way but still see what was happening.

"There's a lot of blood," Dr. Orlean said. "More suction please. I can barely see what I'm doing here." She set the scalpel down on a tray and reached in with her hands. "I've got her. It's a girl. Get ready to clamp the cord."

Dr. Orlean drew the blood-covered baby out. All I could do was stand and stare with wide eyes, feeling stunned and woozy. *Was she all right? Was she alive?*

A nurse carried her to a separate examination table, laid her down and quickly wiped her clean. "She's blue and flaccid."

Everyone moved about in a panic. I felt like I was in some kind of waking nightmare.

"Baby's heart rate's sixty," the nurse said, "but she's unresponsive."

"*Bag and mask her!*" Dr. Orlean shouted from where she stood over Lois, still working frantically to stop the bleeding.

"Still unresponsive," a nurse said. "Heart rate's going down."

"*Start chest compressions!*" Dr. Orlean ordered.

Blind, stark terror rose up in my throat. I was utterly paralyzed as I watched them push with their fingers on top of my daughter's tiny, delicate chest.

Help her! God, please help her!

No one spoke. The air was tense with urgency.

All the sounds in the room—the squeezing of the oxygen bag, the beeping monitors and suction machine—faded to a grim silence in my mind until all I could hear was the thunderous beating of my own heart.

I stared intently at our baby. *Please, little girl, wake up.*

Whoosh, whoosh, whoosh went the oxygen bag.

Then slowly, gradually, her bluish color began to turn pink. Her tiny hand opened and closed.

There was a new sound…a squeak. Then her sweet, beautiful newborn cry filled me with a wave of joy greater than any I'd known in my life.

Thank you, God. Thank you!

Then, like a jolt, I was wrenched out of my joy and thrown back into a dark pool of terror. My gaze swung back to Lois on the table.

Dr. Orlean had sheared the placenta away and was now pulling blood clots the size of fists out of my wife's abdomen.

"We need ten units of PRBCs and FFP," she told a nurse.

I felt woozy again. The room began to spin. The med student must have been keeping an eye on me because she helped me move to a chair in the corner and sat me down. It was all so overwhelming.

Another doctor hurried into the room just then with hands scrubbed and elevated. "What's happening?" he asked as he approached the table to assist.

"I just clamped off the uterine arteries," Dr. Orlean explained. She continued to work but began to shake her head. "This isn't working. It all has to come out."

I glanced up at the student. "What's she talking about?"

"A hysterectomy, I think."

Somehow I was able to rise to my feet. "Wait," I said. "Lois won't be able to have any more children?"

I knew Lois wouldn't want that. We'd often talked about having as many as five.

Dr. Orlean's eyes lifted briefly, but only for a fraction of a second.

"There's no option here, Mr. James. If you want your wife to live, this has to happen."

I realized in that horrendous, shuddering moment that Dr. Orlean wasn't even sure if she could save her.

My eyes shot to Lois's face. She was pasty gray. She looked like death. I could barely comprehend what I was seeing. The mood in the room grew dismal. The gruesome sound of the suction machine made me want to vomit.

This isn't happening. It can't be happening...

"Blood pressure's dropping fast," a nurse said.

"Get the husband out of here," Dr. Orlean firmly replied.

"No!" I resisted when Elaine tried to take hold of my arm. "I need to stay."

"*Get him out!*" Dr. Orlean shouted as she began to work faster to slice and cut.

"BP's still dropping."

"Please, come with me." Elaine grabbed my elbow and pulled me out forcefully. "We can't be in here."

I practically stumbled out of the OR, watching in horror as I passed the operating table and saw more blood spill onto the floor.

Elaine dragged me through the doors. As soon as they swung shut behind me, I pulled the mask off my face and dropped to my knees in the corridor. Burying my face in my hands, I prayed harder than I'd ever prayed in my life.

Please, God. Don't take her from me. Please let her live.

CHAPTER

Three

∘ᴄᴄ⁓ᴐ∘

November 13

E ight hours later, in my sleep, I heard the frightening sound of someone knocking urgently on a window. I woke with a start.

I was slouched sideways in a hard chair in the ICU. It was 6:00 a.m. and I'd been dreaming.

About my oldest sister, Leah.

Leah, a medical resident, had passed away two years ago from complications due to a neurodegenerative disease called ALS.

I was still wracked with guilt over that loss because I hadn't seen my sister in nearly a decade. I hadn't even known she was sick. No one had told me because I'd become estranged from my family years earlier when I was sent to prison for the stupid things I'd done.

In my dream, Leah was in the ICU, looking in at me through the observation window. She knocked hard to wake me, then entered and shook me violently by the shoulder. *"Wake up, Riley! You have to wake up!"*

My eyes flew open and I cried out in fear. *Lois!*

I leaped from my chair and rushed to her side where I found her resting peacefully on the bed. Though she hadn't regained consciousness since the surgery, she was still breathing. The heart monitor was beeping steadily. It was a comforting sound.

I took her hand in mine and marveled at the warmth of her skin which proved there was life—*glorious and beautiful life*—still flowing through her veins. She was strong. She would make it.

Yes…there was hope and joy to be felt here. I knew it in my bones, even though, for a brief moment outside the operating room, I was certain I would lose her. I'd believed she would be taken from me. I'd felt that horrible premonition in my gut.

Then the doctor appeared and told me that Lois had pulled through. Against all odds. She wouldn't be able to have any more children, but she had survived and was in stable condition, and for that I was grateful.

I bent forward and kissed the back of her hand. "Keep resting," I whispered. "I promise I won't leave your side, not even for a second. When you wake up, we'll see our baby girl together and we'll give her a name."

It was a promise I would later regret.

CHAPTER

Four

⌒᥉⌒᥉᥉

"Thank God she's all right," my mother-in-law said when she walked into the ICU a short while later.

I had called her during the night, not long after I was escorted out of the OR. She'd wanted to come to the hospital immediately but I begged her to remain at home with our children. She broke down into a fit of relief and tears a few hours later when I called to report that Lois had survived the surgery.

I rose from my chair to greet Carol, but as soon as our eyes met, I couldn't form words. Neither could she. We stepped into each other's arms and held tightly for a long time.

"The doctor was just here," I said as we moved apart and collected ourselves. "She said Lois is doing fine."

"But she hasn't regained consciousness at all?" Carol asked with concern as she removed her coat and draped it over the chair.

I shook my head. "She lost a lot of blood. Besides that, she was in labor for almost twenty-four hours. Neither of us slept a wink, so she has to be exhausted."

"You must be exhausted too," Carol said, running a hand over my shoulder.

"I've been out cold in that chair for hours," I told her. "How are the kids?"

"Fine. I dropped Danny off at school just now and your neighbor, Joan, is babysitting Trudy. I didn't tell the children anything about what happened. I didn't want to scare them. I promised they could come and visit later."

"It's just as well," I replied. "I don't think they need to know how close they came to losing their mother."

"How's the baby?" Carol asked.

"Fine. Eight pounds, seven ounces." I held up my wrist to show Carol the bracelet that identified me as a new father. "One of the nurses came in during the night and gave me a full report. They asked if it was okay to feed her from a bottle because she was hungry. I said yes. I hope that's okay. Lois won't be happy about that. She wanted to breast feed."

"It'll be fine," Carol said. "She still can, when she's able. She wouldn't want us to let the poor darling starve. Have you gone to see her yet?"

"No, I'm waiting for Lois to wake up. I want us to see her together, and we still have to decide on a name."

Carol leaned over the bed and kissed Lois on the forehead. "Thank goodness everything's all right. I don't know what I would have done…"

My heart rose up in my throat. "Me neither. She's my whole world, Carol. My life was a disaster until the day I met her."

I had been living in L.A. and had just been released from my second stay in prison—a one-year sentence for a DUI that had been reduced to six months for good behavior. Determined not to end up back in jail a third time, I'd finally separated myself from the stoners I'd considered friends and joined a support group for addicts in the basement of my neighborhood church.

Lois worked in the coffee shop across the street and for some reason I'll never quite be able to comprehend, she saw something in me. "Something magical," she always said.

Lois was different from any of the friends I'd had in the past. She was a college girl—smart, kind-hearted, close to her parents. Most importantly, she believed in forgiveness and second chances.

"She changed my life," I said to Carol.

Just then, a young nurse walked into the room and looked around with concern.

"Is something wrong?" Carol asked.

The nurse's cheeks flushed red. "Did someone bring your baby down to you?"

"No," I replied. "I told them to wait until my wife was awake."

She immediately turned and ran out. I felt a rush of alarm and ran after her. "Wait! What's going on?"

The nurse didn't stop. She sprinted down the length of the corridor.

I followed and thrust my arm between the elevator doors just as they were closing, shoved them open and stepped on. "Why are you running?"

She pressed the "close door" button about five times in rapid succession.

"We can't find your baby."

"What do you mean you can't *find* her?"

Her brow furrowed with tension. "She was there in the nursery earlier when we gave her a bottle. Then we laid her down to sleep, but now she's gone."

"*Gone.* I don't understand."

"I'm sure we'll find her," the nurse said, though she was tapping her foot anxiously, her eyes focused intently on the floor numbers as they changed. "Somebody probably took her to the wrong room. Maybe she's back now."

"What the hell?"

The doors opened and the nurse dashed off toward the nursery. I followed closely behind.

Five

⌐ⲥ⤳ↄↄ

"How could this happen?" I asked as I moved from crib to crib and checked the incubators as well. "You can't just lose a baby. Someone must have taken her to another floor. Was she all right? Did something happen?"

"She was fine. She'd been sleeping since she had the bottle." The nurse picked up the phone at the desk and called someone.

"What time was that?"

"Around five," she replied. "She was due for another feeding and that's when we noticed she was gone." The nurse spoke into the phone. "No, the father doesn't have her. He's here with me now."

"Who are you talking to?" I asked, holding out my hand to take the phone from her. "I want to talk to them."

She handed me the receiver. "It's the head nurse. She's down in security looking at the surveillance recordings."

"*Jesus!*" I grabbed the phone. "This is Riley James. Where's my daughter?"

"We're trying to locate her, sir."

"I certainly hope so!"

The nurse spoke in a patronizingly calm voice. "We've notified security and put out an alert. They're searching every floor in the hospital as we speak."

"Have the police been notified?"

"Not yet."

"I'm calling them right now." I slammed the receiver down, pulled my cell phone out of my pocket and quickly dialed 9-1-1.

CHAPTER

Six

༄

I don't believe actual words exist to adequately describe the agony a parent endures when a child goes missing. It's an unimaginable nightmare, a bottomless pit of heartrending, uninterrupted black misery as you torture yourself with images of what could be happening to your child.

You are wracked with guilt and regret over all the little details—like waiting to see your baby until your wife regained consciousness—the things you could have done differently that would have prevented this terrible disaster from happening in the first place. As a parent, you believe you have failed your child. Thinking of her out there somewhere, without your love and protection, is beyond excruciating.

That is where words fail me.

༄

It's safe to say that the hours in the hospital after I spoke to the police were the darkest of my life—and I'd experienced some pretty bleak situations in my younger days. My addictions nearly killed me. I did things I can't even bear to think about. Prison was no picnic, but it was nothing compared to this.

My baby daughter was gone and she didn't even have a name.

I'd also watched my wife come close to bleeding to death on an operating table and I'd faced the clear likelihood of her death. By some miracle she survived, but she had yet to return to consciousness.

When she woke—*and I prayed to God that she would*—I'd have to tell her that the doctor had removed her uterus and ovaries. She'd learn that she couldn't have any more children, and the baby she'd just delivered was gone. Our child had been stolen out of the hospital and I had no idea where she was, or with whom.

I sat next to Lois with my forehead resting on the bedrail, my eyes squeezed tightly shut as I caressed her limp hand in mine.

Please, God...Is this some sort of punishment for my past sins? Haven't I done enough to atone for all that? Or is this some kind of test? Do I still need to prove how sorry I am? What more do You want from me? I thought You'd forgiven me. Why, God? Why this?

In that moment, Lois's finger twitched. My heart beat thunderously in my chest as I lifted my head, opened my stinging, bloodshot eyes and searched her face for signs of awareness.

Her eyes fluttered open. I rose heavily out of my chair to lean over her. "Lois...baby, I'm here."

She blinked up at the ceiling for a few seconds, then turned her head on the pillow and nodded weakly.

Tears filled my eyes as I bent forward to kiss her. *My darling, beautiful wife...Thank you, God. Thank you for this, at least.*

"The baby..." Lois whispered. "Is she all right?"

Carol approached the other side of the bed. "Lois, sweetheart...You're awake. We're so glad."

She met her mother's tearful gaze. "Hi, Mom."

Carol bent forward to kiss and hug her daughter, and I knew there was so much more beneath this woman's calm surface. Like me, she was overwhelmingly grateful for Lois's recovery, yet cognizant of the terrible news we would have to deliver to her—after Lois had already endured so much.

"What happened?" Lois groggily asked. "Did they do a C-section?"

"Yes," I replied, "and they got the baby out. She was okay, but you were losing a lot of blood. You were in bad shape."

"Were you there?" she asked.

I nodded and squeezed her hand. "Of course. It was serious and I was pretty worried, but you pulled through. You were a real fighter, babe, just like always, and Dr. Orlean was amazing. She saved your life."

"Sounds pretty dramatic," Lois said with a tiny smile.

I'd never loved her more.

But the love I felt sent a severe burning dread straight to my gut.

"I'm sorry, but I have to tell you something else," I said, steeling myself to deliver the first wave of the difficult news. "There were some complications with the surgery."

"Is the baby okay?" she asked again.

"The baby did fine," I replied, "but Dr. Orlean had to..." I stopped and looked down. "You were hemorrhaging, Lois. She had to do a hysterectomy. I'm so sorry."

Lois lay still for a long time with her eyes closed, and I worried she hadn't understood what I'd just told her. Would I need to describe all the details? Explain the reasons why? Maybe that would be better left to the doctor.

Then at last my wife opened her eyes, looked at me and spoke. "So I can't have any more babies?"

I shook my head.

Lois breathed deeply and nodded with a quiet acceptance. "I suppose I should consider myself lucky. I'm alive today and I have three beautiful children—children I love. Can I see her?" She was of course referring to our newborn daughter.

Carol's eyes met mine from the opposite side of the bed. We shared a look of painful indecision. *How would we tell her?*

"Not yet, sweetheart," Carol finally said, taking hold of her hand. "There's a bit of a…" She paused and swallowed uneasily. "A situation."

Lois frowned. "What kind of situation? I thought you said she was okay."

"She is," I replied. "She *was,* but…"

"*Was?*" With a flash of concern, Lois tried to sit up, but winced in pain.

"Lois, sweetheart," Carol said as she gently encouraged her daughter to lie back down on the pillows. "You've just had major surgery. You need to stay calm."

Oh, crap…

"Stay *calm?*" Lois exploded with visible agitation. "What's going on? What aren't you telling me?"

I leaned over her. "I don't even know how to explain…It's bad, Lois. The baby was fine after the section. I heard her cry and it was the best sound in the world, but then they had to take her to the nursery while they finished working on you."

She stared at me in horror. "And *then* what happened?"

It wasn't easy to look her in the eye. "Somehow…I don't know how…She went missing from the nursery."

Lois shook her head in bewilderment. "What are you talking about?"

"She was there and doing well," I tried to explain. "They fed her around six this morning, then put her down to sleep. When they checked on her later, she was gone."

"Gone. How can…? What time is it now?"

"Almost nine."

Her panicked eyes darted from my face to her mother's. "They haven't found her? This isn't making any sense."

"I know," I replied. "We're doing everything we can to try and figure it out. The police are here. I told them everything and they're going to want to ask you questions, too. The hospital has been searching everywhere, but it's like she just…disappeared into thin air."

"Disappeared." Lois's face twisted into a mixture of confusion and anxiety. "My baby…Please tell me this is some kind of a cruel joke."

A nurse ran into the room.

My gaze shot like a bullet to the poor innocent health care worker. I knew she had nothing to do with my daughter's disappearance, yet I blamed her just the same. I blamed *everyone* in this place.

"She's awake," I told the nurse. "We just told her what happened."

The nurse approached the side of the bed. "How are you feeling Mrs. James? Are you in any pain?"

"Are you kidding me?" she replied, trying again to sit up. "My husband just told me my baby's missing. I don't care about the pain!"

All the color drained from the nurse's face. "I'll get the doctor."

She bolted from the room.

"I don't understand how this could happen," Lois said to me for the hundredth time after the doctor checked her over and gave her a sedative. "It was the first day of her life, her first moments in the world, and neither of us were there to hold her and tell her we loved her. Why didn't you go as soon as you woke up?"

She laid a hand over her eyes, as if she couldn't bear to imagine it.

"I was so afraid of losing you," I explained. "You almost died last night and I wanted us to see our baby *together* so we could name her. I didn't want to do it without you."

She lowered her hand and gazed up at me pleadingly. "If only you had gone to the nursery and checked on her."

I pressed the heels of my fists into my forehead. *God, help us.* "I know, I know! If I could go back and do it differently, I would. I didn't realize she wouldn't be safe. It's a *hospital.*"

Carol, who had remained silent until that moment, rose from her chair. "Lois, you can't blame Riley. He was awake for almost thirty hours. He had to sleep at some point. We're all on the same side here. We all just want to get your baby back."

Lois listened to her mother's gentle admonishment, closed her eyes and swallowed hard. "You're right. I'm sorry." She opened her eyes and squeezed my hand. "It's not your fault. But how could someone just *take* her? And how will they ever find her?"

"We can't lose hope." Even as I spoke the words, they felt trite and clichéd.

"I can't bear this," Lois said to me. "All I want to do is get out of this bed and do something to find her, but I can't even move!"

I laid my hand on hers but it was a flimsy, inadequate attempt at comfort because I knew nothing could ease her pain except the return of our baby.

"The police are doing everything they can," I tried to assure her. "They understand how important it is to find her as quickly as possible."

She listened for a moment, as if she were trying to cling to a dangling fragment of hope, but could find none.

Carol gave me a sympathetic look, but nothing could alter the fact that I blamed myself for this. Though my wife agreed it wasn't my fault, the helpless, fearful look in her eyes was like a knife in my heart because despite my checkered past, she'd always called me her hero. She'd seen me as a good man. A strong man. She'd helped me believe it was true and that I was worthy of her love and capable of great things.

Today I was furious with myself. Why hadn't I gone to see my newborn daughter? How could I have left her in the care of others for those crucial first few hours of her life? What was I thinking?

Lois looked into my eyes. "We have to find her, Riley. If we don't, I don't know how I'll survive."

I stood motionless in the sterile ICU room regarding the wife I loved—deep in the marrow of my bones—and felt a chill roll through my body. My daughter had been gone for as many as three hours. I wasn't a cop or a psychic. What was I supposed to do? Go outside and sniff the wind?

Lois continued to stare at me fixedly until I nodded. "We'll find her," I said.

Then a detective walked into the room—the same guy I'd spoken with earlier. He wore a dress shirt and black leather jacket. I thought he was in his mid-thirties when I first met him, but this time he looked older than that. I noticed a touch of gray in his dark hair.

"Mrs. James," he said, "I'm Lieutenant Miller. Can I ask you a few questions?"

"Of course," she replied, awkwardly moving to sit up. "And I have a few questions for you, too. I want to know what happened and exactly what's being done."

I decided to listen in. Maybe I'd learn something.

꧁∽⟊⟋∽꧂

Detective Miller asked Lois the same questions he'd asked me, one of which was why we hadn't given the baby a name yet. Lois explained our reasoning rather testily, as if Miller were insulting us as parents, insinuating that we didn't care or hadn't really wanted this third child. Needless to say, Lois put him firmly in his place.

I wasn't surprised when the subject of my criminal record came up again. Did I have any old enemies? he asked her. Did she know if I kept in touch with anyone from my past? Was I using again?

Of course the answers were no, no, and still no. Forever no. The last time I walked out of prison was the end of that life. I'd given up those destructive vices and was determined not to repeat the same mistakes over and over. I had gone to church, joined support groups and returned to school to learn a respectable trade: carpentry. I'd been working in construction ever since and had been promoted to a supervisor's position. I loved my job, my wife, my children, and I hadn't taken a drink or a pill in seven years.

My wife told Detective Miller all of that, but I suspected he'd be poking around my personal business just the same. Though why he thought I'd have anything to do with my own daughter's disappearance was a mystery to me.

Oddly, as soon as he walked out and my mother-in-law moved to take Lois's hand, I felt a sudden sense of purpose. I don't know where it came from, but I presumed it had something to do with the detective's questions about my past.

The notion that my baby daughter might have been kidnapped while in the care of others hit me like a hammer—because my two other children were also currently in the care of others. *Were they safe?*

I grabbed my jacket and ran out.

By the time I pulled into my driveway, I'd already picked Danny up from school and had checked in with my neighbor, Joan, who assured me Trudy was fine. I explained everything to Joan and told her not to take her eyes off Trudy until I arrived.

I walked through the front door, dropped my keys onto the front table and scooped my daughter into my arms.

"Hi Daddy," she cheerfully said in that sweet, singsong voice that always charmed me. Today it knocked the wind out of me. I could barely keep it together. After everything Lois and I had been through, I was running on fumes. I'd hardly slept and my heart was pulsing with an unsettling mixture of grief and rage—at both the world and myself.

"What's wrong?" Trudy asked as I squeezed her tighter than I ever had before and couldn't bring myself to let go.

Quickly, I wiped at the tears in my eyes and set her down on the floor. "I just missed you, that's all."

She giggled up at me. "Where's Mommy? Where's the baby?"

Danny had already grilled me about this in the car. It wasn't an easy question to answer.

"Mommy's still at the hospital," I replied. "She was awake for a long time having the baby, so she's very tired and resting now. We have to wait a little while before we can see her."

Danny dropped his lunch bag and moved past me to play with his toy airplanes in the living room. "And the baby still doesn't have a name," he told his sister.

Trudy swung Polly, her oversized, blue rag doll, around and around in a circle and looked at me strangely. "How come?"

Taking in a deep breath, I strove not to reveal how guilty I felt about that. "We just haven't made up our minds yet, that's all. What have *you* been doing all morning?" I asked, deciding a change of subject might at least buy me some time to figure out how to answer these difficult questions.

"We made cookies."

"Real cookies or Playdough cookies?"

"Real ones," she replied with another giggle.

"Are there any left?" I asked.

She nodded and pointed toward the kitchen.

I turned and saw my neighbor, Joan, standing in the kitchen doorway. At seventy-six, she was an affable woman who dyed her hair red and wore floral leggings, bulky sweaters and colorful scarves. She had grandchildren of her own but they lived in Texas and only visited a few times a year.

Her shoulders rose and fell with a sigh as she dried her hands on a dishtowel. "Any news?"

"Not yet," I replied, wishing this was all just a bad dream.

"You look like you could use a cookie," Joan said. "Have you eaten breakfast?"

"I haven't eaten anything since yesterday."

She gestured for me to follow her to the kitchen.

Trudy hugged my leg and stepped onto my boot. I played along and lugged her and Polly across the hall.

A half hour later, I assured Joan that I was fine with the kids and insisted she go home to her husband, Harry.

"You're sure you'll be all right?" she asked as she gathered her purse and coat from the front hall closet.

"I'll be fine. Carol's with Lois for now, and I need to be here."

"I understand. Call me if I can do anything. I can be here in a heartbeat, day or night."

"Thanks Joan." I said good-bye at the door, then gently closed and locked it.

Turning to look at Danny and Trudy watching television in the living room, I noticed a surreal—almost trancelike—sense of calm in the house, as if everything were perfectly normal and I had not been to hell and back over the past twenty-four hours.

I wished I could be in their heads, just for a moment. To be unaware of the truth. To be sheltered from it.

Moving to the sofa, I sat down to watch *Arthur* with my children. Trudy crawled across the cushions, lay her head on my lap, stuck her thumb in her mouth and hugged Polly.

I stroked her fine golden hair away from her face and thought about my other daughter—the baby with no name—who was somewhere else in the world at that moment.

Where? With whom?

Would I ever see her again in this life?

My stomach churned with acid. The house felt eerily quiet, even though the television blared and Danny kicked his leg back and forth, banging his heel against the upholstered chair in the corner of the room.

Both my children were oblivious to anything but the cartoon on TV. They knew nothing of the physical pain their mother had endured the night before...the blood and the panic in the OR. They felt no fear or dread about their lost sister, of whom they knew nothing. They had no notion of their parents' suffering, and I knew it was our job to protect them from it as best we could.

Or was it?

My thoughts were interrupted by Trudy rolling onto her back, pulling her thumb out of her mouth and looking up at me. "What's the matter, Daddy?"

Somewhat mystified, I blinked down at her. "Nothing's the matter."

"You're sad."

A lump the size of a golf ball formed in my throat. "Why do you say that?"

"Because you're crying."

I felt my eyebrows sink downward. "I'm not crying, sweetheart."

"Yes, you are." With her tiny, four-year-old hand, she poked me in the chest. "You're crying in here."

The earth seemed to shift on its axis. I wet my lips and inclined my head.

"Are you sad about the baby?" she asked.

I glanced across at Danny who was no longer watching television. He was staring at me intently.

Picking Trudy up to sit her on my lap, I slid a lock of hair behind her ear. "What do you know about the baby? Did Joan say something? Or did Nanny call and talk to you?"

"No." Trudy's cheeks flushed with color, as if she'd been caught doing something bad.

"Then what is it, sweetheart? Why do you think I'm sad?"

"Because she's gone."

I felt the color drain from my face. "How do you know that?"

"The lady told me."

I swallowed hard and fought to remain calm as I sat forward slightly. "What lady?"

From the television, Arthur began to sing about library cards. Growing sleepy and distracted, Trudy glanced back at the screen, snuggled down on my lap and slid her thumb back into her mouth.

"The lady who came to the house this morning."

"Danny, do you know anything about this?" I asked my
son.

"No," he replied with a look of alarm.

My heart began to pummel my ribcage. A little too firmly, I
picked Trudy up again and plunked her down in a sitting position
on the sofa beside me. She gaped at me with surprise.

"Who was the lady?" I asked. "Did you know her?"

"No."

"What did she look like?"

Trudy shrugged a shoulder.

"Try, honey. Was she an older lady like Joan? Or young, like
Mommy?"

"Like Mommy."

I began to breathe faster. "What time was it? Was it before or
after Joan came to take care of you?"

"I don't know."

"Please think, Trudy. Try to remember. Was Nanny here
looking after you, or were you with Joan? Was it when you were
baking cookies?"

She shook her head. "I was in my jammies. It was dark
outside."

"So, very early then," I elaborated for her. "Did the lady come to the door? Did Nanny let her in?"

"No. The lady was already in."

"Already inside?" My stomach turned over with sickening dread. "*Where*, inside?"

"In the baby's room. She was standing over the crib."

Though I was screaming inside my head, I fought to keep my cool. "Did you hear something and get out of bed? Or were you up already?"

"I was in bed. I thought it was Mommy. The light was on."

"So you got out of bed and went into the baby's room...but it wasn't Mommy," I added, seeking to understand, encouraging her to tell me more. "What did the lady say to you?"

"I don't know."

I shut my eyes briefly, willing myself to speak in a mollifying voice. "Try to remember, sweetheart. It's very important. Did she know your name?"

Trudy shook her head.

"Was she nice, or mean?"

"She was nice."

I bent my head closer. "Did she tell you *her* name?"

Trudy shrugged again.

This was like getting blood from a stone.

"What did she say to you?" I asked in a more demanding voice. "*Think*, Trudy."

She hugged Polly closer. "She told me not to be scared."

Oh God. "What else?"

"She said she loved the baby. She promised to take good care of her."

My breaths came fast and short. Immediately, I dug into my pocket for my phone, went to the kitchen and called Detective Miller. I told him everything Trudy had just said, word for word.

"Was she able to give you a description?" Miller asked.

"Not yet, but I'll keep trying."

"Don't overwhelm her," he added. "I'm on my way. And don't touch anything in the baby's room. We'll be gathering evidence and dusting for prints. Was there any sign of forced entry?"

"Not that I know of, but I haven't checked around yet."

"Don't touch a thing," he repeated. "We'll do a thorough search. Who was with your children at the time? Was it your mother-in-law?"

"Yes."

"I'll definitely need to talk to her again."

I cupped my forehead in a hand and shut my eyes. "I can't believe this is happening."

"This is good news, Riley," Miller assured me. "It's a solid lead. You should call your wife and let her know."

I nodded in agreement, hung up and prayed this would get us somewhere.

Six Months Earlier

Jenn Nichols

Someone very wise once told me that our greatest purpose in life was to find joy. That seemed rather self-indulgent to me at the time, and I couldn't help but wonder about all the sickos in the world who got their jollies out of hurting others. Surely that should never be someone's higher purpose, under any circumstances.

But that wasn't the kind of joy this person was referring to. She was talking about something else entirely. Something far more pure. It took me a long time to truly understand it, but in the end, I finally got it.

Since I'm about to bare my soul to you, I suppose I should formally introduce myself. My name is Jenn Nichols and I turned thirty a few weeks ago. I've always been a bit of a dreamer, but in a good way. When I was young, I imagined myself doing amazing things like becoming a television reporter who covers wars and weather disasters, or an ER nurse who remains cool headed under pressure and helps people feel safe when they're gravely sick or injured.

When I say I'm a dreamer in a good way, what I mean to suggest is that when I aspire toward something, I feel confident enough in my intelligence and abilities to achieve it. I don't just dream about it. I understand that I have to take action, and I do.

I've always found it rather sad that most of us go through life believing there's plenty of time to make our dreams come true. "Someday I'm going to…" Any goal could be inserted there. You've probably been guilty of that yourself at some point, haven't you?

Or some of us get stuck in a rut and can't stop focusing on the past. We see only the possibility of the status quo instead of looking toward a different future.

Well, I have news for you. Life is short. It flies by faster than you think, and you never know when the rug will get pulled out from under you, so if you really want something more, you need to get busy.

Where do you want to be five years from now? Ten years? Don't just dream about it. Start the ball rolling *now* so that when those years are behind you, you won't still be standing at the bottom of the mountain looking up.

If you're wondering what qualifies me to give advice about goal setting and making your dreams come true, I promise I'll reveal that to you later. But first I want you to know what kind of person I am.

I won't start at the *very* beginning because that would be boring. I'll simply disclose that I enjoyed a normal childhood with one older sister who was sometimes difficult to be around because she was overly dramatic as a teenager and frustratingly pessimistic and surly. She went a bit wild and made some bad decisions, and I now recognize that she may have had some mental health issues, even back then.

As for me, I was always sensible, levelheaded and emotionally content growing up. I was a slightly above average student in high school where I played on the volleyball team. I wasn't gorgeous by any means, but I wasn't hideous either. I didn't struggle with any self-esteem issues. As far as adolescence goes, mine was pretty much a cake walk.

Now let's fast-forward to young adulthood: I went to my local college, graduated with a business degree and wound up working in the human resources department of a retail office supply chain. It was a decent job for a kid fresh out of college.

That's where I met my husband Jake—on the very day he quit. He worked in the printing division but was leaving to join the army.

The physical attraction I felt for him was immediate. He was tall and muscular, with dark hair and giant, deep-set blue eyes. And extremely polite. When he sat down in front of my desk to collect his Record of Employment, I lost my breath. I was only twenty-four at the time and he was twenty-seven, but when he answered my questions, he addressed me respectfully with 'Yes, ma'am.' 'No, ma'am.'

No one had ever spoken to me like that before. There was a quiet charm about him that didn't come across as flirty at all. This was a good thing because, as a rule, I didn't go for the flirty types. I found that kind of behavior superficial and untrustworthy.

But not Jake. He was courteous, reserved, and a little on the shy side. Except when it came time for him to walk out of my cubicle. That's when he stopped, turned around and said, "Would you like to come to my going away party tonight? The staff is taking me out for drinks at the Covered Bridge. You could bring a friend if you want."

I almost swallowed my gum because the corporate office staff rarely socialized with the retail employees—especially those of us in HR.

Trying not to fall off my chair onto the floor, I managed to say: "That sounds like fun. I'd love to come."

The rest, as they say, is history.

When you know, you know.

Things moved quickly after that. We tied the knot a few months after Jake finished boot camp.

The first four years of our marriage were idyllic and lovely. I loved my husband with all my heart and everything was perfect—but then something unexpected happened, and my world began to change.

Twelve

cᴄ◡ᴏ

July 30

"I'm surprised," I said as I rose from the supper table to carry my empty plate to the counter. "I actually thought you might be happy about this."

Jake set down his fork and sat back. "Why would you think that? You know how I feel, and the timing couldn't be worse."

"Is there *ever* a good time to have a baby?" I couldn't even look at my husband. All I could do was stand over the sink and stare down at the drain. "Tell me one person who actually felt ready to be a parent. All parents are scared. Especially the first time."

With a flash of regret, I immediately recognized my blunder because I knew this wasn't the first time—not for *him*, anyway.

Jake's chair scraped across the floor as he stood. "Did you really just say that?"

I sighed heavily and turned to face him. "I'm sorry, but I don't see the point in having this conversation—*again*—when the horse has already left the barn."

There could be no more deliberating, no more discussions about why Jake didn't want a child and how I thought he needed to let go of the past. Whether he liked it or not, I was pregnant and due to deliver in seven and a half months. Besides, I was tired of arguing about it. I'd been pleading my case for two years, working tirelessly to convince him that it would be different this time—that the future could be amazing if he would give it a chance.

Jake regarded me with frustration in the early evening light beaming in through the kitchen windows. "I don't understand how this could have happened," he said. "I thought you were on the pill."

"I am—I *was*—and I don't know how it happened either."

He was quiet for a long moment, and I was relieved he didn't accuse me of getting pregnant on purpose.

"You knew how I felt about this," he said. "You knew it when we got married and you accepted it, for better or worse."

"Yes," I replied, "but I didn't think you'd feel that way forever." I sounded childish, even to my own ears. "I thought you'd change your mind eventually."

He drew back and shook his head as if he couldn't believe what he was hearing. "You agreed you didn't want kids."

"I never said that," I replied, wagging a finger. "I only said I understood how you felt, that it was okay, and that I wasn't ready either. And I wasn't—not at the time—but I honestly believed you'd feel differently by now."

Jake strode into the living room where he began to pace.

I followed him in. "You're angry."

His eyes lifted to meet mine. "Yes."

"Everything will be fine," I tried to convince him. "I can handle this. *We* can handle this."

"You don't know that," he said with a frown. "And Christ, I'm not even going to be here! I'll be halfway across the world!"

We'd known for weeks about his deployment to Afghanistan. He was leaving at the end of the month and would be gone for nine months. It wouldn't be the first time we'd lived apart. He was a soldier and it came with the territory. I'd never complained about it before and I certainly didn't intend to start then.

"I'll have lots of support," I told him. "Mom is less than an hour away and Sylvie is just across town."

He gave me a look. "You think Sylvie will be helpful?"

"Maybe." I hesitated. "I don't know…"

Jake sat down on the sofa and cupped his forehead in a hand. "God, I thought we were on the same page."

"We are. And I didn't do this on purpose. It just happened. I don't know how, but here we are."

He raked his fingers through his hair. "I don't want to do this again, Jenn. I *can't* do it again."

I sat down beside him and laid my hand on his back.

Jake and I began dating five years ago, and early on he took me out to dinner, ordered a bottle of wine and told me he'd been married once before. I was shocked to hear it because he seemed too young to be divorced. Naturally I wanted to know what happened.

He explained that he'd married his high school sweetheart at the age of twenty-one and everything was fine until she got pregnant.

"All I ever wanted was to be a dad," he told me as he poured us each a second glass of wine. "Then Chelsea had a rough pregnancy with terrible morning sickness. It put a strain on our relationship because she was always irritable and I was doing shift work, so I wasn't much better. After the baby was born she started acting differently. At first it made no sense to me because all of a sudden, she's was nothing like the girl I knew. She stopped taking showers and she was crying all the time. She always seemed angry with me, like I couldn't do anything right. She blamed me for the smallest things—like if the corner of the carpet was curled up and she tripped on it, it was all my fault. How could I let that happen? Didn't I care that she might get hurt? Didn't I love her? That kind of thing. I figured out pretty quickly that it was postpartum depression. At least she went to see her doctor about it."

He stopped talking for a moment, fingered the stem of his wine glass and seemed lost in thought.

"I'm sorry you went through all that," I gently said.

He nodded. "Thanks. Anyway...things just went downhill from there."

"How?"

He took another sip of his wine and kept his eyes on the table as he spoke. "One night we went to bed exhausted, which was pretty typical because one of us was always up every couple of hours for bottle feedings—"

"She didn't breast feed?"

"No," he replied, shaking his head, "which was a good thing for me because I got to feed Ava, too, and that was great. I loved doing it. Anyway, we slept like the dead, both of us, all night long. Chelsea woke up when the sun came in the window. She asked if I'd gotten up to feed Ava, but I hadn't, and somehow we both just knew. Don't ask me how. You'd think we'd be happy that our child had slept through the night for the first time, but we both knew that wasn't what happened."

He swallowed hard and sipped his wine again.

"It was SIDS," he added. "We found her...in her crib."

I sat back in my chair. "Oh, God, Jake, I'm so sorry." Neither of us spoke for a moment. "How old was she?"

"Four months."

Taking a deep breath and letting it out, I leaned forward and covered his hand with mine. "I don't know what to say."

He waved a dismissive hand, as if it wasn't necessary for me to say anything because it wouldn't make any difference anyway.

"You didn't want to try to have more children?" I asked after a time.

"Not after living through that nightmare. As for Chelsea, she just wanted out of the marriage. She wouldn't even talk to me. It was like she hated my guts. I think she hated herself, too." He paused. "The guilt...You can't imagine it. You can't help but blame yourself and in your mind you go over and over all the things you could have done differently. Everything you did wrong. You just feel so much anger over how things worked out. What I really wish is that we could have leaned on each other more instead of feeling bitter toward each other."

"You were young," I said.

He nodded and took a breath. "Everything just got so screwed up. I couldn't stop any of it from happening. That was the worst part. I had no control over anything."

As I sat on the sofa rubbing Jake's back, I recalled our conversation from five years earlier and understood completely why he was so frightened about this.

But that was a long time ago—*and I'm not Chelsea.*

"It won't be like before," I assured him. "I promise I'll be able to handle this. And it's highly unlikely that something like that would happen twice to the same family. Think about it this way: The odds are in our favor. But even if it did happen, I'm strong and so are you. I love you more than anything in the world, and no matter what happens, we'll get through it, together."

Jake leaned forward, rapped his knuckles on the coffee table and gave me an anxious warning look. "Please knock on wood when you say things like that."

I immediately leaned forward and knocked.

Later that night

It was sometime after 10:00 p.m. when I knocked hard on my sister's apartment door. "Sylvie! Let me in!"

Jazz music was blaring inside so I knew she was there, but I'd been knocking for the past five minutes and she hadn't answered.

Her hysterical phone call earlier had sent me into a panic and my blood pressure was surely skyrocketing by now. Jake had been called in to work so I had no choice but to hop in the car and drive over there as fast as I could.

Just then, the door across the hall opened and a thin, elderly woman with a cigarette hanging out of her mouth peered out at me. "She's been playing that music for an hour. I called the super but he's not answering either. That girl's going to get herself kicked out of here if she keeps that up."

"I know, I'm very sorry," I replied. "I'm her sister. I'll talk to her."

"If she ever opens the door."

At long last, the safety chain jangled across the track and the door opened. "I was taking a shower," Sylvie explained defensively before I could say a word.

I took in her overall appearance. She wore a blue terrycloth bathrobe and had wrapped a pink towel around her head. Her mascara was smudged sloppily under her eyes.

"Are you okay?" I asked.

"Do I *look* okay?" she testily replied as she opened the door wider and invited me in. Behind me, the neighbor across the hall shut her door.

A moment later, I stood in the tiny kitchen of Sylvie's one-bedroom apartment, watching her pour herself a glass of white wine, full to the brim.

She tossed the empty bottle into a recycling bin with a clatter. "Another dead soldier," she said flippantly.

I bowed my head and took a deep breath, for I was never fond of that expression.

"Want some?" Sylvie asked. "I can open another bottle."

"No, thanks. I'm driving." *Among other reasons.*

I glanced around and took note of the empty Chinese food boxes on the kitchen table—not the kind you order from a restaurant, but the kind you buy frozen at the supermarket and heat up in the microwave.

"I should have seen the signs," Sylvie said, fretfully pacing around the kitchen while she gulped down her wine. "Damn him!"

"How did you find out?"

"Oh, you know…" She casually waved a hand through the air. "He just started acting all antsy and uncomfortable. He said he never meant to hurt me, but I know he didn't care about that. He just wanted to have a good time. At least he took me out for dinner before he dropped the bomb."

She guzzled half the glass of wine.

"So, he never wore a ring?" I asked.

She scoffed at me. "Am I stupid? I wouldn't have gone out with him in the first place if I'd known he was married. He must have taken it off every time he came into the club."

Sylvie was a waitress at a chic dance bar downtown. While we were in college, it was a dream job for her because all her friends went there on weekends and the tips were fantastic. But now she was thirty-two years old and her friends were all married and starting families. It wasn't exactly a healthy environment for someone like her.

"You need to find another job," I said, leaning back on the counter. "A day job where you can meet people who aren't just out looking for a party. Take a course or something."

She shifted her weight and raised an eyebrow. "Really, Jenn? You're going to kick me when I'm down? Start judging me?"

"I'm not judging you. I just think you're in a rut, that's all. A change would be good."

She rolled her eyes, pulled the towel off her head, and flung it onto the back of a kitchen chair. Her long wet hair fell down her back in tangled blond waves.

I noticed at least a half-inch of dark roots, which concerned me because Sylvie was always on top of her hair appointments. She was gorgeous and took great pride in her appearance. The last time I saw her roots showing, she was heading into a severe depression and ended up on suicide watch.

"Oh, hell," she said, tipping her head back. "Maybe you're right. I should get out of there. I'm sick of meeting guys like John. I just don't know what else to do. I never finished college so I'm not qualified for anything except maybe retail. But I couldn't live without my tips."

I followed her into the living room where she continued to pace around. I wanted to tell her to slow down with the wine, but knew I needed to tread carefully to get through to her. I needed to connect and build up her confidence.

"What would you *like* to do?" I asked in a more cheerful, uplifting tone. "Could you see yourself working in an office? You could wear skirts and heels every day, meet smart professional men. It's not too late to take your life in a whole new direction, you know. You're only thirty-two and you're smart. You could do anything you want."

"I can't just quit my job," she argued. "I have rent to pay."

I sat down and patted the sofa cushion beside me. "Let's take this one step at a time. Where there's a will, there's a way."

She let out a heavy sigh and sat down.

"What do you love doing?" I asked. "Let's focus on that first."

She thought about it for a moment, set her wine glass down on the coffee table and shifted to face me. "You know what I love? All those decorating shows on TV. Maybe I could be one of those home stagers for houses that go on sale."

I glanced around her apartment which was tiny but tastefully decorated. "We could definitely look into that. I'm sure there are courses you could take. And you're good with people. You have gorgeous taste. That's obvious from the way you dress and present yourself. I think you'd be amazing at that. Do you want me to Google it?"

I pulled out my phone and searched for some programs she could enroll in. Most of them were six months to a year in duration. Some of them were offered by correspondence.

She picked up her wine again. "I don't know about this."

"Why not?" *Please, Sylvie. Give it a chance.*

"I don't want to do anything by correspondence. Like you said, I'm in a rut. I'd be kidding myself if I thought I could wake up in the morning and break out the books. You know I work late. I need to sleep in the day."

Though she was hesitant, the fact that we were even discussing this was astounding to me. I knew I couldn't drop the ball now. Not while she was actually considering a real change.

Maybe it was a mistake not to think it through, but suddenly I found myself blurting out another option. "What if you moved in with *me*?"

Sylvie inclined her head doubtfully. "Seriously? I don't think Jake would be too happy about that."

"Well…maybe not under normal circumstances, but things aren't exactly normal right now."

"What do you mean?"

Should I be doing this?

A part of me worried about telling Sylvie the truth. It wasn't exactly the best timing after her break up with John. Nevertheless, I carried on.

"No one knows this yet," I said. "I haven't even told Mom, but Jake just found out he's getting deployed to Afghanistan. He'll be gone for nine months, and on top of that…" I paused. "Well…I'm pregnant."

My sister stared at me, expressionless. "Pregnant?"

I forced myself to smile brightly and nod, hoping my joy would somehow reflect back at me. "Yes!"

My news was met with silence. Then Sylvie finally spoke. "That's amazing. Really. But I thought Jake didn't want kids."

I tried to keep the mood light. "It wasn't exactly planned."

She blinked a few times, then at last, she leaned forward to hug me. "Congratulations. I'm happy for you."

"Thank you." I knew my sister too well, however, and felt an emotional thundercloud roll into the room. *Here we go.*

Sylvie rose from the sofa and looked down at me. "Well, this definitely calls for a toast."

With a sigh of defeat, I watched her stride into the kitchen, pull another bottle of wine out of the rack on the counter and hunt around for a corkscrew.

"Here it is," she said to herself as she opened a drawer. With trembling hands, she pulled the cork out with a *pop*. Still seated on the sofa, I was surprised when she poured me a glass.

"I can't drink that," I reminded her.

She stopped, set the bottle down and let out a silly laugh. "Oh, what an idiot. Of course you can't. That sucks. Cheers anyway."

Raising her own glass, she took a deep swig, then glanced around the kitchen as if she were searching for something, but didn't know what it was.

I rose from the sofa and joined her. "Jake's going to be gone for a long time. I could really use your company, Sylvie. It would be good for both of us because I don't want to do this alone. You could get out of your lease, quit your job and live with me rent free until you get back on your feet. Think about it. You could go to school and take whatever kind of course you want. It would be a fresh start, and you wouldn't be alone either."

Her gaze dipped to my belly, which was still as flat as a pancake. "I don't know, Jenn. I'm not sure I could handle being around you."

I swallowed uneasily. "Why not?"

She scoffed. "You *know* why." She gestured toward my belly.

Of course, I understood that she was referring to the abortion she'd had when she was sixteen. The two of us had always spent our summer holidays with our grandparents on the coast of Maine, and during one exceptionally hot summer, Sylvie fell fast and hard for a handsome eighteen-year-old. She didn't find out she was pregnant until October, after we'd returned home to Montana and gone back to school.

She still considered that boy from Maine to be the great love of her life. Unfortunately things didn't work out for them.

"I always wanted babies," she complained to me, "but look at my life now." She glanced around her apartment. "It might really depress me to see you pregnant in *your* perfect life."

I strode closer. "Just so you know, my life isn't all roses and sunshine. Jake's not exactly happy about this, and I'm really worried about him going away for so long. But that's not the point. What matters is that a change like this could really turn things around for you, open up new opportunities you never imagined."

There it was—my unstoppable optimism. My belief in something better just around the bend. If only she could see life that way, too, but sadly she was crippled by regret. She limped along through life because she couldn't let go of the past.

Sylvie backed away to lean against the counter and regarded me with a look of cool derision. "I'll think about it, Jenn, but don't clear out the guest room just yet. I can't make any promises."

"Great," I said with forced enthusiasm, finding it difficult to meet her resentful stare. I glanced around for my purse. "Take some time to think about it. I should probably go."

She said nothing as I walked out, and I wondered how Jake was going to feel about all this.

Not good, I suspected.

I was in bed with the lights out when Jake returned home after midnight. Hearing the key in the door, I tossed the covers aside and padded in my bare feet to the kitchen where I found him standing in front of the open refrigerator.

"There's some leftover spaghetti from yesterday," I said, striding forward to help him find it at the back of the fridge. "There it is." I moved the milk and juice around to get my hands on it. "Here you go."

As I held it out to him, I realized he was staring at me intently. Deep stress lines creased his forehead.

Jake and I had always been immensely close; we never fought. Our marriage was solid as a rock, but suddenly I was frightened for the future. A shiver moved through me.

He closed the refrigerator door. Without a word, he took the plastic container out of my hands, set it on the counter and faced me.

"I'm sorry," he softly said. "I've been a jerk."

Feeling completely dumbfounded, I shook my head. "No, you haven't."

"Yes, I have. When you told me you were pregnant, I reacted like…" He stopped and took a moment to compose his thoughts. "I was an ass. What's weird about it is that I always wanted to have kids and be a dad. That's the life I imagined, with a woman just like *you*. Then everything went wrong with Chelsea. The whole idea became...I don't know. *Tainted*."

I still didn't know what to say. I wasn't sure where he was going with this.

He took my hand, raised it to his lips and kissed it tenderly. "I love you more than anything in the world, Jenn, and I'm happy about this. Really, I mean it. I want to have this baby with you. I want us to be a family."

A cry of relief broke from my lips and I pulled his hands to my mouth to kiss them, over and over. He wrapped his arms around my waist and held me against his strong body. All the doubts and fears of the past few days flew away as I breathed in the familiar scent of him. My husband, whom I loved with all my heart and soul.

"I'm so sorry," he said again, burying his face in my neck and laying kisses there. "I promise I'll be a good dad. I just wish I didn't have to leave you. I don't want to miss this, and I don't want you to be alone."

Drawing back slightly, I looked up at his face in the glare of the kitchen lights and laid my open palm on his cheek. "You won't miss it," I said. "I'll post pictures online every day. I was thinking about it, and we can do video chats. We'll be in contact with each other constantly."

He touched his forehead to mine. "It won't be the same if I can't touch you and hold the baby when he comes. Or she, if it's a girl."

I smiled as a warm, loving glow spread through my body. "The time will fly by and she'll barely be three months old when you come home. Think how incredible that will be. Everything will be great and..." I stopped for a moment, wondering if I should tell him about Sylvie now or wait until I was certain she was actually coming.

"What is it?" Jake's brows pulled together with a look of suspicion. It was impossible to hide anything from him.

Backing away, I moved to heat up the spaghetti. "I got a call from Sylvie tonight," I explained as I peeled the lid off the container. "John just broke up with her."

"Uh, oh…" Jake replied ominously. "Was she all right?"

I shrugged. "Jury's still out on that one."

"How long did it take you to talk her off the ledge?" he asked.

I slid him a knowing look as I placed the spaghetti container inside the microwave, set it for two minutes and pressed start. "It was touch and go for the first twenty minutes on the phone. She wouldn't stop crying, so I went over there. Surprisingly, once I got there, she seemed to have pulled herself together. I talked to her again about going back to school or getting a new job and for the first time ever, she actually seemed keen on the idea."

"Really? That's a switch."

"Tell me about it."

Jake sat down at the table. "Do you think she'll actually do something like that?"

"Well…" I reached into the cupboard for a plate and set it on the counter. "I sort of made her an offer."

Jake looked at me with trepidation. "What kind of offer?"

"I suggested that if she wanted to quit her job at the bar and take a course to get a diploma in something, she could move in with me while you were gone. To save money."

His eyebrows lifted. "You invited her to live here? For nine months?"

The beeper went off and I opened the microwave. "I know, I know. I'm still not sure if it was the brightest move, but I really want to help her, Jake. I just want her to be happy, and even though things are fine now, I'll probably need some help later on when I'm as big as a barn and I can't rake the lawn or carry the garbage out. And I'd like to have someone here for when I go into labor and need to get to the hospital."

Jake thought about that for a minute or two. "Would you make her your birthing partner?" he asked. "I thought you might ask your mom."

I filled a glass with water at the sink. "I hadn't even thought about that. I'm still working through issues like getting Sylvie out of her lease or helping her figure out what kind of program would be good for her. And who knows? She might not even want to come. You know how she is. She doesn't handle change well."

I served the hot spaghetti onto the plate, sprinkled some parmesan cheese on top and carried it to the table with the water.

Jake picked up his fork to dig in. I sat down across from him.

"What did she say when you told her you were pregnant?" he asked knowingly, lifting a brow.

I let out a sigh. "She congratulated me of course, but I could tell she was shaken up. She wasn't expecting that."

We both knew that deep down, Sylvie had never gotten over the heartbreak of her first love and the abortion she later came to regret. Jake was no stranger to her emotional ups and downs. He'd been there at my parents' house when she went upstairs to the attic in the middle of a family dinner. The next thing we knew, she was lugging a box of her childhood toys outside to set fire to it—because clearly, in her mind, she was never going to be blessed with children of her own.

"Do you think she'll be able to handle seeing you go through a pregnancy?" he asked.

"She doesn't have much choice. Whether she lives with me or not, it's happening. But I honestly believe it'll be easier on her if she can get her act together. She just needs to feel hopeful about something. Feel good about herself and the future, instead of focusing on the past."

"What she needs is therapy," Jake added coolly as he twirled the spaghetti noodles around his fork.

Maybe I was a fool—and too optimistic for my own good—but I genuinely believed that if my sister moved in with me, I'd be able to help her.

Interestingly, it didn't turn out that way. Not even close.

Riley

November 13

"**G**ood news." Detective Miller walked into the kitchen where I was standing at the counter, drinking coffee. "Lieutenant Holmes was able to glean a few more details from your daughter. It's not much, but it's something."

Holmes was a female detective who, no doubt, had a gentler touch than I did. She was still in the living room with Trudy—playing Barbies—while a team of investigators were making their way through the house dusting for prints. Others were outside talking to neighbors.

I set my coffee cup down on the counter. "What did she say?"

He consulted his notepad. "She described the woman as tall, slender with brown hair in a single ponytail. She also described a tattoo on the inside of her forearm, which tells us she may not have been wearing a coat."

"A tattoo?" That didn't sit well in my mind. I'd known too many guys in prison with tattoos. "Was she able to describe it?"

Miller hesitated. "She's only four so her descriptions aren't exactly articulate. From what we can gather, it's possibly a word, about seven to ten letters long, but she wasn't able to tell us what it said."

"She can't read yet," I explained, "but she knows her alphabet. We have a wooden alphabet puzzle. If Lieutenant Holmes wants to give it a try, Trudy might be able to identify some of the letters she saw."

"That would be helpful. Can you get it?"

I went into Trudy's room to find the puzzle on her bookshelf, returned to the kitchen and handed it to Detective Miller, who called Holmes into the kitchen.

While Holmes resumed "playing" with Trudy, I went to check on Danny, who was in his room with his portable Nintendo device. "You okay, buddy?" I asked.

He set the device down and sat up on the bed. "Are the police going to find her?"

I moved fully into the room and sat on the edge of the bed. "They're doing everything they can. All we can do is stay positive."

"What do you mean?"

I squeezed his shoulder. "Think good thoughts. Say prayers. And we need to take care of each other."

"I already said a prayer," Danny replied, reaching for a sheet of paper on the bed beside him. "I even wrote it down, like a letter." He handed it to me. The words were simple, written in light blue marker.

Dear God,

Please take care of my baby sister and help us find her soon. I promise to be good.

Danny James

"This is wonderful," I said. "I'll do the same thing."

I handed the paper back to him but his eyes remained downcast. He was quiet for a long moment until at last his eyes lifted. "Why didn't you tell me when you picked me up at school? Why did you lie?"

My stomach dropped and I swallowed uncomfortably. "I'm sorry, Danny...I didn't mean to lie. I just didn't want to scare you and I was waiting for the right time to tell you and Trudy. I thought maybe we'd find your sister first and then everything would be okay, but you're right. I should have told you."

He sat forward and hugged me. "I'm scared, Dad. What if they take me and Trudy, too?"

I held him tight. "They won't. I promise. Everything's going to be okay. I won't let anything happen to you."

But after what happened to my newborn daughter, could I live up to that promise to my son?

Holmes was still working with Trudy when I realized I hadn't called my family in Boston since very early that morning. The last time I'd spoken to my mother, I was still waiting for Lois to wake up and I hadn't even learned that our baby was gone.

Since then, I'd been ignoring my mother's calls. Maybe I hoped we'd find our daughter before I'd have to deliver the news. Or maybe I was just ashamed that I hadn't prevented this from happening. Thoughts of what my father would say about it grated through my nerves like sharp steel teeth—because he and I were on shaky ground to begin with. I dreaded the assumptions he would make. He might suspect I sold my daughter for drug money, or that an enemy from my prison days was out for revenge...

For all I knew, he could turn out to be right.

Knowing I had to face this hurdle eventually, I called my mother's home phone number.

"Hello?" she answered. "Oh, Riley, thank goodness. We've been so worried. How's Lois? How's the baby?"

I sat down at the kitchen table and lay my head in a hand. "I don't know how to tell you this, Mom. You better sit down."

I waited until she replied. "All right. I'm sitting. You're on speaker phone now. Holly's here, too."

Holly was my younger sister. She was in her final year of med school and had recently married one of my childhood friends—Josh Wallace, a Boston police officer.

I proceeded to explain what had happened that morning before Lois woke up and described everything that was being done to find our daughter.

"I can't believe this," my mother quietly sobbed. "Dear Lord. How could that happen?"

"I don't know. The hospital's in a ruckus. I suspect it'll be on the local news tonight."

"Have you called a lawyer?" my mother asked. "Because this is above and beyond unacceptable. Someone clearly wasn't doing their job."

"Suing the hospital isn't exactly at the top of my priority list right now," I replied. "I just want to find our daughter."

"Of course, of course." She sniffed and said nothing for a few seconds. "I have to come out there, Riley. I can't just sit here and do nothing. I'll stay in a hotel if you don't have room at your house."

"I'll come too," Holly added.

"You have school," I reminded her. "And we're doing everything we can here. The police are on top of it."

"I'll tell Josh about it as soon as we hang up," Holly said. "I don't know if there's anything he can do from here, but he might have some advice for you."

"Thanks," I replied. "And Mom, if you want to come, we could use your help. There was some mention of setting up a call center and getting the community involved to get the word out. Handing out flyers, that sort of thing."

"I'll book a flight right away," she said. "I should get there tonight."

Just then, Detective Miller entered the kitchen and looked at me. He held up his notepad, as if he had some important new information to convey.

"I gotta go," I said. "Call me when you know what time you'll be arriving." I set my phone down on the table. "What is it?" I asked. "Did you learn something?"

"Yeah," he replied. "Something interesting."

"We tried the puzzle," Detective Miller said, striding closer. "Your daughter wasn't completely sure. She seemed a bit hesitant, but she said she thought the woman's tattoo was letters followed by numbers. She also mentioned there were two dots on top of each other—most likely a colon—and a horizontal line which was probably a dash."

"She didn't pick out any of the letters or numbers?" I asked.

"She was able to identify an 8 and a 4, and a J at the beginning. She said she thought it was a word with four or maybe five letters."

I let out a breath and bowed my head. "That doesn't tell us much. What could it mean?"

"We're looking into it," Miller replied. "It could be someone's birthday or anniversary."

Lieutenant Holmes entered the kitchen. "I just had a light-bulb moment. What if it's a bible citation? They're usually listed by book, chapter and verse, in that order." She pulled a pen and notepad out of her pocket and wrote down an example. "Like this." She held it up: *John 3:16–17*

I stared at it intently. "So this might suggest that the kidnapper is religious? Go figure."

"Call it in," Detective Miller said. "We'll have someone search for all the passages with a J, 8 and 4."

Lieutenant Holmes dug her phone out of her pocket while I went to the living room to spend some time with Trudy.

⸺❦⸺

That afternoon, Miller returned to the hospital to question my mother-in-law about the intruder. He then called back to report that Carol, who had remained at Lois's bedside all morning, was shocked to learn of it. She explained that she had risen from bed at 7:15 a.m. without hearing a thing. Trudy hadn't mentioned it to her either. Both Lois and Carol were disturbed by the news and I spent a half hour on the phone with Lois, promising I would keep a close eye on our other two children.

Still needing to do something proactive while I remained at home with them, I set them up with a movie in the living room while I went online at the kitchen table to do a search on infant kidnappings. After an hour I felt nauseous. There were so many missing children. The cops were searching for a needle in a haystack.

Shutting down the computer, I checked on the kids, then sat down on the edge of my bed and did nothing but fiddle with the hospital band on my wrist. The numbers on it connected me with my newborn child. It identified me as the father. Lois wore the same bracelet, and our baby wore one on her ankle.

Was she still wearing it? I wondered miserably, needing to look away.

The sick churning in my stomach continued. My pulse throbbed in my veins. It wasn't easy to sit still. My fingers tapped rapidly on my knee. I wanted to get up, run out the door and do something that would make a difference. Or lose myself in a drink…

Seven years.

Seven years sober…

If there was ever a moment I was in danger of taking a drink, this was it. Shutting my eyes, I took a few slow, deep breaths, then re-shifted the focus of my thoughts away from me.

A few minutes later, I was back at the kitchen table, flipping through the family bible, searching the scriptures for verses with the letter J and numbers 8 and 4 in the headings. I read for a long while, but nothing jumped out at me as a clue about the kidnapper.

I recalled what Detective Miller had said about the woman not wearing a coat. It was the middle of November. Had she simply taken it off when she entered? Or did she leave a warm car running outside in the driveway? If so, why wouldn't Carol have heard it?

In the end, I read recommended verses for those in need of comfort until I nodded off at the table with my head resting on my arms.

CHAPTER

Seventeen

‿ᴄᴄ⌒ᴏᴏ‿

Later in the afternoon, Carol returned home to watch over Trudy and Danny so that I could return to the hospital to visit with Lois. I arrived to discover they had moved her out of the ICU to a private room, which was good news in terms of her recovery.

Physically, she was doing well. Mentally was another story altogether. I almost didn't recognize her when I walked in the room. Her eyes were puffy from crying and her skin was blotchy. As soon as our eyes met, she asked desperately, "Did they find her?"

I shook my head solemnly. "Not yet." Approaching the bed, I kissed her and held her for a long time. "The police were at the house for hours this morning. They have some good leads. Trudy was able to give them a description of the woman, and the tattoo is definitely something to go on."

"You said you thought it might be a bible citation?"

"Maybe," I replied. "We don't know for sure, but they're looking into it. I spent the afternoon reading scriptures. Looking for a clue."

"Did you find anything?" she asked hopefully.

"Not yet."

Lois looked up at the ceiling and sighed. "Maybe you should bring Trudy in here so I can talk to her. I might be able to get more information out of her."

"We could try, but Lieutenant Holmes was brilliant with her," I assured my wife. "She worked with her for quite a while. Played with her, actually."

Lois turned her head on the pillow to look at me. "Still…I'm her mother."

A feeling of love and understanding moved between us and I prayed that somehow the collective love we felt for our missing daughter would count for something. We wanted her back so desperately. Either one of us would walk through fire for her. I would give my right arm to have her back. I would die for her…for any one of our children.

Backing away from the bed, I sat down in the chair by the wall.

A nurse came in to take Lois's temperature and blood pressure. While I sat there considering how powerless we both were in that moment, I began to feel agitated and restless. I looked around the hospital room and realized suddenly that they hadn't brought Lois to the maternity floor to recover from her C-section. We were on some other floor—where we couldn't hear the sound of babies crying.

It was not where I'd imagined we'd be today, but I was glad for it.

Rain pelted the windshield as I drove home from the hospital. I kept the wipers pumping at full speed across the glass and ran the defrost fan on high, which made it impossible to hear the radio. Nevertheless—hungry for local news—I tried station after station and cranked up the volume. Eventually I shut off the radio and told myself that my phone would ring if there were any developments in the case. Surely, Miller would call.

Continuing to drive through the stormy city which was congested with rush hour traffic, I glanced in the rearview mirror at the empty car seat in the back. Lois had asked me to install it weeks ago so we'd be ready to take our baby home after we were discharged.

Oddly, there was something sinister and disturbing about the sight of it over my shoulder. I felt as if the seat itself were judging me with its emptiness.

My guilt and frustrations mounted. Sure enough, like some sort of magnet, my eyes were drawn to a sleazy-looking tavern I passed along the way. How long had it been since I set foot in a place like that? Who would I see there? Anyone who knew me?

Stopping at a red light, I found myself actually contemplating the idea of sneaking into a corner liquor store in a distant neighborhood to pick up a bottle of vodka. If I did that, I'd have to hide it somewhere in the house.

But no, I couldn't let myself fall into that trap. If I purchased a bottle, I'd drink it until it was gone.

Just *one* drink. That was all I wanted. Something to take the edge off.

The light turned green and I drove on, checking my rearview mirror constantly, tapping my thumb on the steering wheel. My stomach muscles clenched tight with tension and I shouted a few obscenities at the car ahead of me.

When the hell would I hear from Miller again? What was happening? Were they doing anything? Anything at all?

The traffic seemed to be moving as slow as molasses. I laid on the horn, checked my mirrors again and swerved into the next lane. Someone honked at me but I didn't care. I cut in front of an SUV and turned sharply into a small parking lot. I pulled to a halt, shut off the engine and looked up at the sign on the building.

JOE'S TAVERN

For a long moment I sat there with the keys in my hand, my heart pounding like a hammer while I worked out the logistics of this. One drink. Just one. A cheap whisky I didn't even like. I'd down it in a single gulp and walk out, and that would be the end of it.

I could do it. Just one and no more after that—just for today because this was the worst day in the history of my life, and that was saying a lot because I'd experienced some pretty bad days.

Letting my eyes fall closed, I searched through all the dark and shadowy alcoves of my mind, working to summon up a few of those old memories—the worst of the bunch—things I'd worked hard to purge over the past ten years.

Why did I want to think of them now? Was I hoping to drown out the noise of the hell I was in today, or was this some quietly heroic attempt to remind myself of the hell I would revisit if I inched any closer to that slippery, whiskey-flooded slope?

Eyes still closed, I recalled the night I broke into my father's house after he'd kicked me out for the umpteenth time. My loser buddies and I—three stoners who all had abusive drunks for fathers and nowhere else to go—were searching for liquor or money or anything else we could get our hands on to sell—so that we could buy more liquor or drugs, or maybe just pay for a pizza.

My father wasn't a drunk, however. He was a brilliant and highly regarded surgeon in Boston who'd saved hundreds of lives. My sisters and I had been raised in a beautifully restored Victorian mansion in a high-end neighborhood with old money and fancy cars. We had the privilege of attending private school and flying south for the holidays every year.

Unfortunately, however—with all those privileges came the highest of expectations, and sadly I could never quite live up to them. Oddly enough it was my two sisters who turned out to be "chips off the old block." They both aspired to careers in medicine while all I ever wanted to do was scramble out from under his thumb and escape my life in that house.

I squeezed my eyes shut tighter as I relived the moment he came down the stairs in the darkness and found us rifling through his liquor cabinet. The next thing I knew I was ducking under the swing of a baseball bat, only to rise again and feel it connect with the left side of my skull. The world spun circles in front of my eyes and the pain reverberated like thunder in my head. We fought like animals and I punched him in the head. He knocked me to the floor, sat on top of me and punched me across the jaw, numerous times. My head bled like a gushing geyser onto his luxurious Persian carpet which I later learned my mother had to replace.

Later, in court, my father claimed he didn't know it was me—that he thought I was some dangerous, anonymous hoodlum. I'll never know for sure if that was the truth, because I remember looking straight into his fiery eyes as he punched me.

What followed was my painful recovery in jail, unaware of the fact that I'd soon be wearing ankle irons and standing before a judge to receive a five-year prison sentence. The funny thing was...*I couldn't care less*. I was glad, in fact. I was immensely pleased with myself for disappointing my father so profoundly. So magnificently...

No, I said to myself as my eyes flew open. *This is a mistake. Seven years. Don't screw it up now.*

I inserted the key into the ignition and started the car, looked over my shoulder to back out. I was about to press on the gas when something stopped me.

The empty car seat in the back.

All my blood rushed to my head. Suddenly, in a flash of movement, I shut off the engine again, unbuckled my seatbelt as if it had caught fire, and left the car.

The next thing I knew I was breathing in the foul scent of musty carpets and stale beer. Quickly, I approached the bar and slid onto a stool.

"What can I get ya'?" the barkeep asked.

"Jack Daniels," I replied. "Two ounces. No ice."

"Coming right up." He set a short tumbler on the bar and poured the amber liquid. I stared, entranced, as it gushed, glistening, into the glass.

My breaths came fast and short as I relived the nightmare of that morning, when panicked, I'd chased after the nurse, followed her onto the elevator and searched all the cribs and incubators in the nursery, hunting for my daughter.

Our newborn was not to be found. *Where was she? What was happening to her at this very moment? Was she even alive?*

My heart beat thunderously as I picked up the glass, swirled the liquid around for a long, slow moment, then closed my eyes and breathed in the familiar intoxicating aroma.

I jumped when my cell phone rang in my pocket. It was my sister, Holly.

I reached for it, swiped the screen and raised the phone to my ear. "Hello?"

"Hi, it's me. Any news?"

"None since Trudy told us about the tattoo," I replied as I set the glass down on the bar and swiveled around on the stool to face the opposite direction.

"That's too bad. Listen, Mom, Josh and I got a flight out of Boston earlier today. We're in Denver right now for a quick layover and are about to board. We should be there in a couple of hours. I don't know how much help we can be. We just want to be there for you."

"Thanks, Sis," I replied, pinching the bridge of my nose and feeling more grateful than she could ever know. "I'll fix up the basement for you and Josh, and Mom can have Trudy's room. I'll move her in with Danny. It'll be good to have you all here. I could definitely use your support."

"You'll have it," Holly replied. "Oh, I gotta go. They're calling for us to board."

I hung up, took a deep breath and swiveled back around on my stool. For a few shaky seconds I stared down at the drink in front of me. The need for it seemed less urgent suddenly. I didn't want to go backwards—*not back there*—so I took advantage of that brief window of resistance and fished in my pocket for my wallet and a few bills to pay for the drink. I tossed them onto the bar, gave the bartender an apologetic shrug and walked out.

On my way home—still needing to do *something* to take the edge off—I stopped off at the hardware store to purchase extra locks for the house and battery-operated alarms for the doors and windows. I assembled and affixed everything as soon as I arrived home—all the while thanking God for that well-timed phone call from my sister.

Jenn
Three Months Pregnant

CHAPTER

Nineteen

Jenn Nichols

I must be honest here. I can't neglect to admit that when I was swimming around in the depths of despair—suffering from an endless, incapacitating case of morning sickness—I felt horribly guilty for assuming that I would be the one carrying my sister Sylvie on an emotional level.

Maybe it was hormones. Or the fact that my husband was in a faraway country fighting a war against an enemy I couldn't even comprehend. Days would sometimes go by where I wouldn't hear a word from him. He wouldn't answer my emails or comment on a photo I posted. Terror would bubble up inside me and I would fear the worst.

Or maybe it was the simple fact that rising a few inches from my horizontal position on the bed at 6:30 in the morning was enough to make me hurl. Unfortunately I had no choice in the matter. I had to get up and go to work. As soon as my feet hit the floor, I'd sprint to the bathroom so I could make it to the toilet in time.

Through all of this, Sylvie was there…bringing me crackers, water, or a bucket, if necessary. She held my hair back when I bent over a garbage can in public; she did my laundry, cleaned the floors and took my car in to have the oil changed.

Sylvie did all these things while starting classes at the local community college where she was studying to become a dental hygienist.

Yes, she was finally getting her act together.

Though I felt sick to my stomach most of the time, I was grateful for that and incredibly proud of my sister. At least for a while. I only wish life could have cooperated. I wish everything *had* unfolded like a fairy tale.

I can't help but wonder why bad things happen the way they do.

September 16

"Hey, baby," Jake said, talking to me from my laptop's screen.

At the sound of his voice, my heart leapt.

"How's the belly?"

"Belly's doing great," I replied with enthusiasm. "I'm still puking my guts out, unfortunately, but everyone keeps telling me it's a *good* sign. It means all the pregnancy hormones are in proper working order. But I also have a bad case of what they call pregnancy brain."

"What's that?"

"Basically, in layman's terms, it makes you stupid. Seriously Jake, I can't believe how absentminded I've been lately. Yesterday I locked the keys in the car, and I just can't seem to multi-task at work like I could before. I get distracted so easily."

"Did you get back into the car?" he asked with concern. "Where were you when it happened?"

"I was at work. Sylvie picked me up and I took the spare set in the next day. It wasn't a problem, just a minor inconvenience."

"That's good to hear. I wish I was there with you."

"Me, too," I replied. "I really miss you."

We gazed at each other in silence for a few seconds, and I felt a wave of melancholy as I considered how far apart we were, but

I didn't want to focus on the negative. I didn't want to waste this precious time grumbling about what couldn't be changed.

"So what happened this week?" I asked with a forced smile. "I didn't hear from you."

He shook his head. "I can't talk about that, babe. Sorry. We were safe though. I can promise you that, at least."

I hated feeling so disconnected from him, so out of reach. All I wanted to do was climb into the computer screen and wrap myself in his arms.

"You look tanned," I mentioned, working hard to keep the mood light and positive. The last thing I wanted was for him to feel guilty or worried about me, when *he* was the one in danger every day.

"We've been outside a lot," he replied, rubbing the top of his head. "Good thing we wear helmets or I'd have a really bad burn."

I smiled. "You're staying away from the Pina Coladas, I hope?"

He laughed. "Don't worry about that. I'd never hear the end of it if I started sipping umbrella drinks around the base."

Though we were both laughing and joking, I knew we were avoiding the real truth—that we were desperate for each other, and his return seemed light-years away.

Of course he knew I was struggling to get through each day, worrying about whether or not he was going to get shot or blown up. All this, while I was throwing up half the time. The stress was ever-present, but at least I was rational enough to accept that I'd signed up for this. I knew he was a soldier when I married him, so I had to accept this as part of my life.

"Is the neighbor's dog still pooping on our lawn?" Jake's question jerked me out of my thoughts. I realized I'd been staring at the wall.

"Funny you should ask," I replied returning my gaze to the laptop screen. "I picked some up yesterday."

"Did you really? You know, I was thinking about ordering you one of those fancy pooper scoopers from the pet store. They're spring loaded with a long handle so you wouldn't even have to bend over."

I considered that. "Sounds intriguing. Might come in handy when I begin to get fatter. But you know how I love that warm squishy feel in the plastic bag."

He laughed. "Stop, baby...You're turning me on. What bag did you use yesterday?"

I narrowed my gaze seductively. "One of those thin white ones from the meat department."

"Oh, God. And what were you wearing?"

"Gray sweatpants."

"You're killing me here."

We both laughed.

"How's Sylvie?" he asked.

"Great."

His eyebrows lifted doubtfully.

"Seriously," I added. "I'm amazed at the change in her. Maybe it's just the fact that she's getting to bed at a decent hour every night and she's up early to help me out and get to class. She's also going to yoga three times a week. It's all helpful and productive."

"And she's okay about...?" He paused. "You know. The baby?"

I nodded. "Actually, she's been really good about it. I think the fact that she has something else to focus on, other than herself, has made a huge difference. She likes her classes and her teachers and she's already talking about applying for a job downtown when she's finished. Get this..." I leaned closer to the laptop screen and spoke softly. "She's growing her hair out. She ditched the bleached-blonde look and had it darkened back to her natural color."

"I don't even know what that is," Jake replied.

"Brown, like mine."

He sat back. "Wow. I can't picture it."

"I know, right? It's like imagining Pamela Anderson as a brunette."

Just then the floorboards creaked in the hall. I raised my forefinger to my lips. "Shhh…"

Jake sat quietly.

I heard the bathroom door open and close. Water ran into the tub.

"It's okay," I whispered. "I don't think she heard anything. She must be taking a bath."

Jake leaned forward in his chair to speak close to the computer microphone. "Just be careful around her, okay? She may seem great right now, but remember, she's the queen of mood swings."

Someone tapped Jake on the shoulder. He stood up so I couldn't see him. Barely audible words were exchanged while I waited uneasily on the bed.

He sat down and faced me again. "Sorry babe, something's come up. I gotta go. Will you post more pictures tomorrow?"

"Of course."

"The pictures help," he added, staring at me uncertainly. "Because I worry about you. And the baby."

"I'm *fine*," I assured him, leaning closer to the camera lens. "Please don't worry, Jake. This is the good stuff. This is what you're supposed to be happy about. I promise we'll be fine. Stay safe."

"Always. And listen, when I get home, let's plan a vacation. Maybe we could take the baby to that seaside cottage we rented for our honeymoon. The one by your grandparents' place in Maine. We've always wanted to go back there. I can't stop thinking about it. I'm so sick of the desert. It's so dry and dusty here. I'd love to get back on that boat."

"That sounds amazing," I replied. "I'll look into it." I blew him a kiss, waited for the screen to go blank, then shut my laptop.

An hour later, wrapped in nothing but a towel, Sylvie knocked on my open door.

I closed my book and sat up in bed. "Hey," I said.

"Hey," she replied, walking in. "How's Jake?"

"He's doing all right. He couldn't tell me where he was the past few days, or where he was going tonight, but he promised they were safe. Those are just words, though. Stuff you're supposed to say."

She moved deeper into my room and sat down on the upholstered chair by the window, crossed one long leg over the other. "That's always the way, isn't it? You never know what he might be doing."

Not wanting to think too much about that, I nodded and regarded her in the dim, golden lamplight. Her shoulders rose and fell with a heavy sigh, as if she were preparing herself for battle.

"I heard what you said about me," she mentioned.

My stomach suddenly dropped. I was immediately filled with regret. Why had I said those things?

"Really Jenn?" Sylvie continued. "Pamela Anderson? Is that how you see me?"

My lips parted. "I'm sorry. And no, it's not how I see you."

She glanced toward the window. "I suppose it's not that far off the mark. It's probably how John saw me, and every other guy who came into the bar and hit on me."

"You're a beautiful woman," I reminded her.

"Mmm." Her gaze met mine like a laser beam. "But I'd like to be more than that."

"You are," I assured her. "Look at what you're doing. You're turning your whole life around. Starting a new career. That's not an easy thing."

Sylvie twirled her hair around a finger. "Tell me about it."

Her gaze dipped to my belly and I saw a look I hadn't seen since before she moved in with me. There was something darkly envious and seething about it.

"You feeling okay tonight?" she asked. "You're not sick or anything?"

"I'm fine," I replied, though I found myself rubbing my temple because this conversation was stressing me out. I still felt terrible that she'd heard me talking to Jake about her hair. It was giving me a headache.

She frowned and leaned forward. "You sure you're all right?"

I lowered my hand to my side. "I have a bit of a headache, but it's no big deal. I don't want to take anything for it."

She tugged at her towel to keep it from falling off as she stood. "No, of course not. Let me know if you want some herbal tea or something. I'll be up for a while."

"Thanks."

She walked out of my room.

I opened my book to continue reading.

CHAPTER

Twenty-one

September 17

I didn't do it often, but I decided it was time to take a sick day at work. For once, I wanted to enjoy the luxury of lying in bed until the nausea passed, which usually happened around ten or eleven. I'd still feel sick after that, but at least the vomiting would stop.

My boss understood, so I slept late and slid out of bed slowly, carefully, sometime before noon.

Slipping into my bathrobe and slippers, I shuffled to the bathroom and managed to brush my teeth and wash my face without needing to hurry to bend over the toilet. This was indeed a remarkably good sign. Everyone kept assuring me the morning sickness would pass after the first three months. I was still waiting for that, but today gave me hope.

As I stared at myself in the mirror, however, all my usual optimism drained out of me like a sieve, straight down to my toes. If death had a face, it would look exactly like mine.

My complexion was pale and ghostly; dark circles underscored my tired, sunken eyes; and my cheeks were sunken and gaunt. Even my lips lacked any pinkish color.

Did I really look this horrendous on a daily basis? What about the pregnancy glow I was supposed to be enjoying? Was that some kind of myth? There was nothing the least bit radiant about me that morning. I looked as gray as a stone, thin and withered. Terribly unhappy.

I supposed I'd been throwing up so much lately, I'd lost a few pounds instead of having gained anything. What I really needed to do was try and eat more—though I couldn't exactly be held responsible for the fact that when I did put something in my mouth, I couldn't keep it down.

With a resigned sigh, I unzipped my makeup bag, dug around for some concealer and blush, and applied some makeup. It didn't help. When all was said and done, I realized I'd put on too much blush. I looked like a clown.

Tugging a tissue out of the box by the sink, I wiped at my cheeks, then tossed the tissue into the waste basket.

I froze as something caught my eye—something in the trash, buried beneath the tissues and a clump of hair Sylvie must have scraped off her hairbrush.

Slowly bending forward, I reached down to withdraw a framed photograph from the basket. As I turned it over, I was shocked to discover it was the picture of the seaside cottage and sailboat Jake and I had rented for our honeymoon in Maine. It had been the most romantic week of my life and he had spoken of it the night before. Now the glass in the frame was shattered and it had been shoved down to the bottom of the trash basket and covered with soiled tissues.

Twenty-two

❝Mom? I'm so glad you answered." I switched the phone from one ear to the other as I stood at the kitchen table, trying not to cut myself as I removed my treasured honeymoon photo from the broken frame. I held it up to the light and examined it closely to make sure it wasn't irreparably damaged. I realized it represented all my hopes and dreams from that incredible first week of my marriage. There had been so much love, so much joy…

"What is it, Jenn? You sound upset."

"I am. I can't believe what just happened."

"Tell me."

I lifted the lid of the garbage can under the sink and tossed the empty frame into it. "I stayed home from work this morning," I explained.

"Oh no. Are you sick again?"

"I haven't *stopped* being sick," I replied. "I just wanted to stay in bed for once. I can't believe how tired I am. Anyway, I got up a little while ago, and when I went into the bathroom, you'll never guess what I found in the garbage."

"What?"

I began to pace around the kitchen. "The framed picture of the house and sailboat Jake and I rented for our honeymoon. You know the one?"

"The one that sits on your mantle?"

"Yes, exactly. You know how much it means to me. Well, the glass was smashed. It looked like it was thrown against a wall or something."

My explanation was met with silence. "Mom, are you there?"

She cleared her throat. "Yes, I'm here, but I don't understand. What are you saying?"

I sat down and buried my forehead in my palm. "First, I should back up a little and tell you about my online chat with Jake last night. We were talking about Sylvie and I said a few things I shouldn't have."

"What did you say, Jenn?"

"It's not really that important," I replied guiltily. "I might have made a comment about her blond hair, and Jake may have said something about her mood swings."

"Oh no. Did she hear you?"

"Yes. She came in afterward and talked to me. I apologized of course and I thought everything was fine until..." I glanced toward the window. "Until I woke up this morning and found this broken picture in the garbage. It was so upsetting, Mom. I can't even tell you."

"That's awful. So you think Sylvie is responsible?"

"Who else would be?" I replied. "She must have been listening to us talking about going back there with the baby when Jake gets home. He mentioned he's sick of the desert and I said I'd look into it."

"You think she heard that, too?"

I shut my eyes and nodded my head. "She must have. And I thought she was doing so well. She seems to love her classes. She's always telling me how good she feels and she thanks me for letting her stay here. Have you talked to her lately? Has she seemed okay?"

There was a long, tell-tale pause. "I've had a few conversations with her...yes."

Instantly I knew I was being kept in the dark about something. I could read my mother like a book. "What's she been talking to you about?"

"She usually calls me during the day, from school."

I digested this information, stood up and went to fill the kettle to make some herbal tea. "Is everything okay with her?"

"I promised I wouldn't say anything," Mom replied ruefully. "She's trying so hard to be supportive of you."

My stomach turned over with dread which created a burning sensation in my core.

"She's been having a hard time lately," my mother continued, "thinking about the baby."

"*My* baby?" I asked.

"No, *hers.*"

Setting the kettle on the stove to boil, I fought with a commotion of conflicting emotions. Part of me was sympathetic toward my sister—for the pain and regret she felt over a choice she'd made in her youth. A choice she could never undo.

Another part of me wanted to grab hold of her and shake her. *It was fifteen years ago, for pity's sake. It's time to let go of the past and move on. Life's too short. Stop punishing yourself!*

I couldn't say any of that, of course. It would be insensitive.

Maybe I was. Maybe I had a heart made of cold, hard steel and that's why I could cope with my husband being deployed to Afghanistan while I was pregnant with the child he hadn't wanted me to have.

"Are you still there, Jenn?" my mother asked.

"Yes, I'm here," I replied, feeling frazzled and realizing I'd blanked out again, become lost in thought.

"I think you should definitely talk to Sylvie about it," Mom said. "You can't just let her get away with something like that. We all understand that she's hurting, but she needs to deal with it like an adult."

"Jake thinks she needs therapy," I said flatly.

My mother grew quiet. "Well…she didn't want me to tell you this either, but I think you should know. She started seeing someone shortly after she moved in with you, and she's trying out some medications."

Incredibly surprised to hear this, I shook my head as if to clear it. "You're kidding me. Why wouldn't she want me to know?"

"You know Sylvie. She's proud, and she's embarrassed because you're her baby sister, yet you've surpassed her in every way. Sometimes Jenn…I know you don't mean to, but you make her feel like a failure."

"What!?" I turned the stove burner to high. "All I ever do is tell her she's great and I do everything I can to help her. Besides, what's that old saying? 'No one can make you feel inferior without your permission?' She can't blame me for her own shortcomings."

Angrily, I reached for the box of tea in the cupboard and slammed it down on the counter.

"And your pregnancy…" Mom added. "Well, maybe that's the straw that's finally breaking the camel's back. You know how badly she's always wanted a child of her own."

"Too bad she didn't feel that way when she was sixteen." Feeling suddenly guilty for my lack of sympathy, I closed my eyes and counted to ten. "I don't want to break her back," I replied soberly. "I don't want to cause her pain, but if my pregnancy is what is making her get help, then maybe that's a good thing."

"That's what I've been telling myself," Mom said. "Let's just hope she can stay strong over the next few months, because she's going to have to get through this. We all have to support her, Jenn. We have to make sure she's all right."

When I hung up the phone, I couldn't help but feel a wave of resentment toward my sister. We all had to support *Sylvie*? What about *me*? I was pregnant and sick with a husband half way around the world fighting a war in Afghanistan. Didn't they watch the news at night? Didn't they know what was going on over there and how dangerous it was? I was constantly terrified he would never come home.

Maybe for once it would have been nice if Sylvie had stepped out of the "pity me" limelight and propped *me* up for a change. Apparently that wasn't in the cards.

⌐⌐c⌐ɔ⌐ɔ

The situation with Sylvie and my perpetual morning sickness left me feeling distinctly fatigued all day. I was at least glad I'd taken the day off work because I could barely get up off the couch.

When at last my sister walked in the door at 4:00 p.m., I was impatient and irritable. It was partly my own fault because I'd worked myself into a tizzy all day, feeling angry about a lot of things and knowing I had to confront her about the broken photo frame in my trash can. I couldn't keep walking on egg shells around her.

"Hey," she said, dropping her backpack on the floor in the front entryway and heading straight for the bathroom.

I waited for the sound of the toilet flushing and the water running before I rose to my feet and made my way to the kitchen, where she was sure to go next.

A moment later, I stood in the doorway watching her bend over for something inside the refrigerator. "What do you want for supper?" she called out, thinking I was still lying on the sofa.

"I'm not really hungry at the moment," I replied.

Her head popped into view over the open door. "Geez, you scared me. I thought you were in the living room."

"I was, but now I'm not."

She stared at me and frowned. "You look terrible. Are you feeling okay?"

"I'm fine," I replied, "except for the fact that I had to dispose of some broken glass this morning. To be more specific, my honeymoon picture was smashed." I folded my arms at my chest and raised my eyebrows. "Do you have anything to say about that?"

A slow wave of antagonism darkened her expression. She glared at me and shut the refrigerator door. "No."

"You don't know anything about that? Nothing at all?"

She merely shrugged.

Her cavalier response grated up and down my spine and I found myself wishing I'd never tried to help her. I should have left her in that sleazy bar to keep making stupid choices and continue screwing up her life. She was a grown woman. She wasn't my responsibility. I had my own problems to deal with.

She, too, folded her arms at her chest. "I honestly don't know what you're talking about."

"No? I think you do."

She scoffed and walked out of the kitchen, stormed down the hall to her room and slammed the door, hard.

There was a sudden pounding sensation in my ears and my vision grew cloudy. Normally, with Sylvie, I always found a way to be gentle and patient. When she was in a state like this, I would do everything in my power not to upset her further—but rather I'd try to calm her down, no matter how long it took, by making her feel safe and loved. She always opened up to me, eventually.

But something was different today. Maybe it was pregnancy hormones. Or maybe I was just sick and tired of enabling her emotional outbursts and irrational behaviors. Unable to stem my anger, I followed and banged on her door.

"I talked to Mom today!" I shouted through the door. "She told me you were seeing a therapist! It's a good thing, too, because you *definitely need help*!"

I had never in my life spoken to my sister that way.

I heard the sound of floorboards creaking from inside, then the door whipped open. "Listen to you. Little Miss Perfect." She shook her head bitterly and spoke in a taunting, sing-song voice. "Because you're so strong and I'm so jealous of you and your perfect marriage that I *hate* myself. *Go to hell, Jenn*!"

The door slammed in my face, and I squeezed my eyes shut to withstand the throbbing exasperation that was spinning around like a tornado inside my brain.

I returned to the sofa and sank onto it.

A few minutes later, Sylvie's bedroom door opened. She stormed out, grabbed her backpack off the floor and said, "I'm going out. Don't expect me home until late."

"Fine," I replied, and went to grab my laptop to call Jake.

Twenty-four

I was fighting tears by the time my husband's image appeared on the screen, which was disturbing on its own because I was not the crying type.

"What's wrong?" he asked, looking shaken. "Is the baby okay?"

Waving my hands in front of my face, I dismissed that notion as quickly as possible. "It's not that," I replied. "The baby's fine. I just had a fight with Sylvie."

His shoulders slumped with relief—or maybe it was empathy for my situation. I wasn't sure.

"What happened?"

"She did something crazy, Jake." I reached for a tissue, tugged it out of the box and blew my nose. "Remember, the other night, when we were talking about her mood swings and her hair color?"

"Yes."

"She came in later because she heard everything."

"Oh, crap."

"I told her I was sorry, but this morning I woke up and found the picture of our honeymoon cottage smashed and stuffed in the bathroom garbage."

Jake's eyebrows pulled together in dismay. "You're joking. You think she put it there?"

I nodded. "I certainly didn't put it there myself. Mom told me she's been seeing a therapist since she moved in here and she's been trying out some medications, so that's good news at least, but this is really upsetting. I don't know what to do."

"What does your mom say?"

"You know how she is. She's always sympathetic toward Sylvie. Sometimes I'm tempted to fall to pieces and screw my life up royally, or throw a temper tantrum, just to get a little attention from her."

He reached forward and adjusted the screen of his laptop. I felt as if he were reaching out to stroke my arm. "But that wouldn't be you," he said. "You could never be a screw up, Jenn. You're steady as a rock. You're stronger than any woman I've ever known and that's why I love you."

I fought to pull myself together. "I don't feel like a rock at the moment. I feel like a giant sack of bruised, mushy pears. I don't understand this. It must be the pregnancy. It's making me crazy."

He chuckled softly. "You'll feel better soon." Then his expression grew stern. "Where is she now?"

"I don't know. She stormed out."

He sat back and rubbed the back of his neck. In that snug gray T-shirt, he was an impressive figure of a man. Muscular and broad-shouldered. I couldn't believe how badly I missed him, how desperately I wanted him with me, just to touch him and be held by him.

"It's lucky for her that I'm in another country right now," he said, "because I'd like to tear a strip off her. I know she's your sister, but I won't have her treating you like that." He leaned forward over the desk. "I hate being so far away from you. I don't want you to have to put up with this kind of crap. Not now."

I nodded in agreement.

"Do you want me to talk to her?" he asked.

"No, I can handle this."

He chewed his lower lip, pondering what I'd said. "I know you can, but you always go really easy on her. I just don't want her to think she can get away with that stuff, especially when you've done so much for her."

"I certainly wasn't easy on her tonight," I told him. "That's why she left. She must have been in shock. She's used to curling up in a fetal position while I stroke her hair, but I totally lost it."

He leaned forward over the desk. "I wonder if it's the new medications that are having an adverse effect. You don't think she'd do anything worse than that, do you?"

"Worse than breaking a photo frame? Like what?"

"She did try to kill herself once," he reminded me. "Remember...she sliced her wrists open with a steak knife. That's kind of violent."

I thought about that for a moment. "She's never tried to hurt anyone other than herself, and let's not be too hard on her. She's finally getting her life together and getting help. She seems to really like the program she's in."

Jake frowned and shook his head. "Two minutes ago you were furious with her. Now you're defending her. Are you feeling all right?"

I let out a frustrated breath. "I'm fine. It's just...my mind feels frazzled lately. It's so hard to focus on things."

"Just keep your eyes open and keep in touch with your mom," he replied. "Tell her everything that Sylvie does. Maybe you should write it all down as it happens so you have a record of it."

"That's a good idea," I replied. "I'll do that tonight."

"Just make sure she doesn't find it," Jake cautioned me. "That might really push her over the edge."

September 18

The following day I arranged to meet Sylvie at the park at lunch hour to talk about our big blow up. She hadn't come home until after midnight the night before, which heightened my anxiety and left me tossing and turning in bed all night. I feared that without my love and support, she might slip back into her old habits of going out to bars on weeknights and becoming involved with men who weren't good for her.

I couldn't help myself. As much as I wanted to take a step back and let her live her own life and make her own mistakes, I continued to feel responsible and protective of her. She was my sister. I loved her and I didn't want to see her get into trouble.

"Hi," Sylvie said coolly as she found me on one of the park benches across from the play structure, which was crawling with preschool-aged children. She was sipping on a large green smoothie she must have purchased somewhere.

Sylvie sat down beside me. I finished my submarine sandwich, balled the plastic wrapper up and set it on the bench for the time being.

"I suppose you want to talk about what happened?" Sylvie said.

"I just want to make sure you're okay," I replied. "That *we're* okay."

For a moment she watched a young mother push her daughter on a swing, then she dropped her gaze to her lap. "I don't know what to say, Jenn. You really threw me for a loop yesterday."

"Why? Because I accused you of smashing my honeymoon picture?"

She shook her head. "That, among other things. You haven't exactly been yourself lately."

"*I* haven't been myself? I admit, sometimes I can get a little hormonal, but I don't think that's the problem we're having." I paused a moment. "Mom told me you've been seeing a therapist."

Sylvie sighed with defeat. "Mom has a big mouth."

"Why didn't you want me to know? I think it's a *good* thing."

Never taking her eyes off the young mother with her little girl, Sylvie squinted through the sunshine, saying nothing.

"I wish you'd talk to me about it," I finally said. "I want to be helpful."

"You are being helpful," she replied. "You got me out of my job and helped me get into this program I'm in. I appreciate all that, I really do, but there's another side to this." She met my gaze directly. "You know what I'm talking about. It's not easy for me, and I need you to accept that. Just let me deal with it in my own way."

"Do you mean the fact that I'm having a baby?"

Sylvie looked away. "Yeah. It kind of rubs salt in the wound— you know what I mean?" She took a moment to gather her thoughts. "I still want to be a mom, but I'm not sure that's ever going to happen. I still feel like I'm being punished or something, that I deserve this."

I nodded in understanding.

"I'm sorry if I'm not being supportive enough," Sylvie added, "but I'm doing my best."

"You're doing *great*," I replied in my usual manner of always making an effort to build up her self-confidence. "And maybe what we argued about yesterday wasn't your fault. Mom also told me you were trying out some medications. Is it possible they might have some strange side effects that cause unusual behavior or blackouts?"

She darted an accusing glance my way. "You're suggesting that I smashed your honeymoon photo and don't remember doing it?"

"It's possible. Maybe you should ask your doctor."

She raised her smoothie and sipped through the straw. "Fine, whatever. I'll ask," she replied bitterly. "But I don't want to have this conversation again, all right? Let's just move on."

Regarding my sister in the harsh noonday light, I wished there was a way I could take away her pain, somehow reverse time to when she was sixteen and convince her to keep her baby—or at the very least put it up for adoption.

"Okay," I said, not wanting to torment her any further.

We both looked up when a small boy screamed in pain after landing on his face in the sand at the base of the slide.

"Did you see that?" Sylvie said. "He went down head first."

"Poor little guy." I noticed a woman on another bench run to help him. "That must be his mom."

The woman picked him up, propped him on his feet, wiped the dirt off his face and hugged him. He continued to wail, regardless.

"I think he's okay," Sylvie said, rising to collect my garbage from lunch. She carried everything to the trash can on the other side of the play structure while I sat and watched the mother tend to her son.

A moment later I found myself rising to walk over to the baby carriage she had left behind at the bench. I peered inside at a tiny infant dressed in pink, sleeping soundly.

"Aren't you beautiful," I cooed, reaching down to touch her soft cheek with the tip of my finger. She stirred and let out an uncomfortable gurgle, then squirmed and grunted. "Do you have a sore tummy?" I asked. The next thing I knew, I was reaching in to pick her up and lift her over my shoulder. I bounced at the knees and patted her on the back as I started walking back to the bench. "Sounds like you need to burp, that's all."

Suddenly, a woman shouted from the play structure. "*Hey! Hey!*"

I was shocked when the mother of the little boy who had fallen off the slide grabbed hold of my arm and glared at me with venom. She tried to snatch the baby from my arms. "Let go of her!"

"Be careful!" I cautioned as I maneuvered to hand the child over.

"Are you crazy?" the woman asked with wild eyes. The baby was now screaming and her son was crying, gripping at her jeans.

Sylvie came running. "What's going on?"

Without a word, the mother turned and stalked off with her two children, pushing the carriage bumpily over the grass.

"Did you pick up her kid?" Sylvie asked in horror.

"She seemed uncomfortable," I replied. "Like she had a gas bubble or something."

Sylvie frowned and scolded me harshly. "You can't just pick up people's babies in playgrounds. *What's wrong with you?*"

"I was only trying to help," I argued.

Sylvie shook her head at me. "Whatever. I have to get back to school. See you at home." She, too, stalked off, leaving me standing alone.

"I was just trying to help," I said to no one but myself as I headed back to work.

Twenty-six

November 8

"I thought it would be Sylvie sitting beside me for this," I said to my mother. "Thanks for coming with me." We sat down in the waiting room in the obstetrics unit. I'd just reached the twenty-week mark and had come in for a scheduled ultrasound. "I really wanted her to be a part of this. I thought it might help her work through her feelings, but here we are."

"You two still aren't talking?" Mom asked.

"Oh, we talk," I replied as I leaned forward to pick up a magazine. "About the weather and how her day went at school. She asks me if I need anything at the grocery store when she goes, and I offer to throw some of her laundry in the machine with mine when I'm doing a load, but as a whole, it's pretty icy in the house, if you know what I mean."

Mom touched my shoulder. "You've always been very forgiving with her, Jenn, but she crossed the line when she broke your honeymoon picture, didn't she? No wonder she won't admit to it, not even to me."

"We'll get over it," I said, waving a hand. "I'm not going to keep banging on that door. She's in therapy so that's all I could ask for."

The nurse appeared with a clipboard and called my name. Mom stood up with me.

"You have the video camera?" I asked over my shoulder as I followed the nurse to the examination room.

"I do. Right here in my purse. You'll be able to show it to Jake tonight."

⸺ઈ⸺

"I hope you don't mind if my mom films this," I said to the nurse as I raised my feet into the exam table. "My husband's out on some kind of mission right now, otherwise I'd have him on a live video feed."

"We've done live feeds many times," the nurse cheerfully replied, smiling up at the camera my mother held. "Sometimes couples just can't get their schedules to match up."

"You don't have to record anything yet, Mom," I whispered to her. "Wait until the doctor comes."

"Oh. Sure." She fumbled with the device and lowered it to her lap.

Just then, Dr. Matthis entered the room and set my chart on the counter. "Hi, Jenn," she said.

"Hi, Dr. Matthis. This is my mother, Patty."

They shook hands. "Nice of you to come." She gave me a playful look. "A little bird tells me you want to know the gender today."

With my hands folded protectively over my belly, which still seemed very flat to me, I turned my head to the side to watch Dr. Matthis take a seat on the rolling stool. "Yes, we definitely want to know. Mom, you can start filming now."

My mother raised the camera again while I did my best to ignore it. I didn't want to come across as awkward or self-conscious.

Meanwhile Dr. Matthis picked up the gel bottle and squirted it noisily onto my belly. "How's the morning sickness been lately?" she asked in a more serious tone.

"Much better," I replied. "I haven't thrown up since...I'm not sure. It's probably been awhile."

"That's good news. No doubt you have some calories you need to catch up on."

"For sure. It was pretty bad in the beginning, but my appetite's finally come back."

"And you're still working full time?" she asked as she slid the probe in a small circle just below my navel.

"Yes."

"Great." She seemed distracted as she watched the screen, then turned the volume up on the fetal monitor to listen for the heartbeat. Static filled the room.

"How have you been feeling otherwise?" she asked, leaning away from me to press another button on the machine.

"Really good," I replied.

She continued to move the probe around while I watched the video screen with bated breath. Turning to look into the camera, I whispered to Jake, as if in private: "I can't believe we're going to know if it's a boy or a girl today. It's crazy, isn't it?"

I slid my gaze back to the screen and waited for the doctor to settle on the image. Since we'd done this before, at ten weeks, I had a pretty good idea what we were looking for.

Static from the monitor continued. The doctor moved the probe further to the left and right.

Time slowed to a surreal pace. Why was this taking so long? My heart began to pound.

Eventually, Dr. Matthis leaned forward and shut off the machine. She turned to face me, pulled a tissue from the dispenser and wiped the gel off my stomach. "Are you sure you've been feeling all right since I saw you last?"

"Yes."

"Have you noticed any spotting?"

"No," I replied with obvious concern in my voice.

Dr. Matthis wet her lips and stared at me uneasily for a few seconds. "I don't know how to tell you this, Jenn." She covered my hand with hers. "I'm afraid you've lost the baby."

Suddenly I was panting as if I'd just run an uphill marathon. I shot a quick gaze at my mother and spoke curtly. "Turn the camera off."

She immediately lowered it and fumbled to find the stop button.

"That can't be true," I said to the doctor. "I've been sick in the mornings, but otherwise, I've been fine. I would have noticed if there was bleeding. There wasn't."

"Are you sure?" she asked. "There would have been significant cramping as well."

I shook my head. "No, nothing. Can you try again? With another machine? Maybe this one's broken."

Dr. Matthis regarded me with sympathy, then instructed the nurse to bring in another ultrasound machine.

A moment later, we were repeating the same procedure with a smaller, portable unit. I kept waiting for the beautiful, rapid whirly thrum of the baby's heartbeat, but heard only a steady stream of static. The doctor searched and searched, moving the probe over my belly until I began to weep quietly.

"I don't understand," I said, pressing my palm to my forehead. "I thought we were fine."

The doctor shut everything off again. "I'm so sorry, Jenn."

The walls seemed to close in all around me. I felt like I was losing my breath. My mother moved to hold me in her arms while I struggled to grasp the heart-crushing fact that I'd lost the baby I'd wanted so desperately. The baby I'd loved and dreamed about.

Heaven help me. How would I ever tell Jake?

That night, while I lay in bed in total darkness and silence, hugging a pillow and staring at the wall, my mother baked cookies in my kitchen. It was a generous but regrettably hopeless attempt to offer comfort because I was convinced that nothing could ever pull me out of this funk.

I still didn't understand how any of this could have happened. That very morning, barely eight hours earlier, I'd been sitting at the kitchen table with my hand on my belly, waiting eagerly to feel the baby kick for the first time, which I'd expected to happen any day.

A gentle knock sounded at my door. My body seemed made of lead. Somehow I managed to roll onto my back. "Come in."

The door opened and light spilled across the floor. I squinted as my pupils adjusted.

"Hey," Sylvie said. "How are you feeling?"

"Like I've been hit by a truck. And I have a pain in my head. Right here." I pointed at my forehead.

She nodded with understanding. "Mind if I come in?"

"As long as you promise not to turn on the light," I replied. "I don't want to look at the world. It hurts."

Sylvie entered but left the door open a crack. Sitting down on the edge of my bed, she stroked my hair away from my face.

"I'm sorry, Jenn. I know there's nothing anyone can say to make it better. I just want you to know that I understand and I'm here for you, whatever you need."

"Thank you." I swallowed over a painful lump in my throat that rose up out of nowhere.

"I don't know what to do," I confessed. "I feel so lost. It's like somebody just ripped my heart out and stole my whole life, my future, right out from under me."

Sylvie shifted slightly. "Would you like me to tell Jake for you? If you're not feeling up to it?"

"Tell him what?" I asked, glancing at my alarm clock. "We usually chat at midnight." That was two hours from now. I sat up against the headboard, ran my fingers through my hair and took a deep breath. "I feel gross. I can't let him see me like this. I should take a shower."

"You look fine," she assured me while staring at me intently. "And no one expects you to be a hundred percent right now. Not after what you've been through."

Wringing my hands together on my lap, I said, "What I've been through...? That's right. Oh God."

*The baby...*I inched down on the bed and covered my face with my hands.

"How am I going to tell him? I know what he'll say. He'll say, 'See? I told you this would happen.' And I don't want him to think he has to carry me emotionally. He went through that before with his first wife. She couldn't get over losing their baby. She got really depressed and blamed him, and I don't want to be pathetic like that. You're pathetic like that, too." I stopped myself. "Oh, God, did I just say that? That was so insensitive."

What was wrong with me?

My sister looked down at her hands. "Yeah."

Neither of us said anything for a moment or two. Then Sylvie's eyes lifted. "Depression's not something you can control, you know. Sometimes it's a chemical imbalance or it's hormonal. It can happen to anyone at any time. Even to you, Jenn."

Not wanting to argue with her, I lowered my gaze. It's not that I disagreed. I knew it could happen to anyone; I just didn't believe it would ever happen to *me*. I'd always been incredibly rational and self-disciplined. I remained calm in a crisis when everyone else around me was in a panic—because I was in control of my mind and therefore my emotions. I almost never let them get the better of me.

Well…the pregnancy hormones had caused a few changes, but I refused to consider that the same thing.

But still, I understood what she was trying to tell me—that I had to be more forgiving and understanding when others were suffering.

"I'm sorry I've been so hard on you lately," I said. "I've had my own stuff going on. Know what I mean?"

"Of course." She twirled the birthstone ring around on her finger. "I want to talk to you about that, actually."

Recognizing my sister's hesitation, I regarded her curiously.

When I gave no reply, her eyes lifted again. "Do you still have no idea when you lost the baby?"

Our neighbor's dog began to bark outside in their backyard. I glanced toward the open window. Then, without warning, something urgent and insistent compelled me to rise from the bed to close it.

After I shut it tight, I flicked the locks and noticed a thick layer of dust on the sill. Moving to my dresser, I pulled a tissue out of the box and wiped the sill clean. Then I threw the tissue into the wastebasket. I noticed it was full, and picked it up.

What's this wrapper from? Feeling suddenly agitated, I reached into the basket and withdrew a colorful plastic candy bar wrapper. "Were you in here eating chocolate?" I asked Sylvie with a frown. "Were you snooping around or something?"

"No," she replied defensively. "Why?"

"Because I didn't eat this. I hate this kind of chocolate. It has nuts in it."

With growing apprehension, my sister shook her head at me. "I never came in here to eat chocolate."

Just like you never broke my honeymoon picture?

"Please come back and sit down," Sylvie pleaded while patting the bed. "I want to finish talking about this."

"About what?"

She blinked at me a few times. "About what happened. You didn't answer my question. Do you still have no idea *when* you lost the baby?"

"Lost the baby…?"

This confused me. What was she talking about? Then my stomach dropped sickeningly as I recalled sitting on the examination table in the clinic that morning. I remembered the static on the monitor, the doctor's concerned expression, my mother fumbling in a panic to shut off the camera…

Overcome with a sudden wave of grief and a terrifying burst of fear in my veins—*what was happening to me?*—I set the wastepaper basket down on the floor. "No."

As I returned to the bed and climbed onto it, I couldn't help shivering at the troubled expression on my sister's face—as if I were sprouting horns.

"Jenn…" she cautiously said, "do you think it's possible you might be suffering from some memory loss?"

I couldn't deny that there had been many instances over the past few weeks where I'd felt confused and disoriented, easily distracted. Like just now, when I heard the dog barking…

Sylvie inched a little closer. "Remember the day when I came home from school and you accused me of smashing your photograph?"

I nodded.

"You looked really bad that day. You were white as a sheet and you'd called in sick that morning. Do you remember making the actual phone call or *why* you made it?"

I struggled to think. "Yes. I felt sick, like I always did in the mornings, and too tired to get out of bed."

"Do you recall anything before that? Why you were so tired? Is it possible you might have had the miscarriage during the night?"

I fought hard to remember. "I slept all morning. It was noon when I got up. But if I miscarried, there would have been blood."

Sylvie nodded. "Yes, there would have been, unless you cleaned it up, or it happened in the shower or something. But the spotting can go on for days. Surely you would have noticed." She paused when I cupped my forehead in a hand. "What is it? Do you remember something?"

I labored to locate details in my mind, but it was like trying to make sense of images from an illogical dream that comes to you later, hours or even days after you wake up. "There might have been some bleeding…but I thought I'd dreamed it. I remember not thinking anything of it. I just told myself, 'That's weird. I must be having a period.'"

Sylvie touched my knee. "When was this?"

"I don't remember. Maybe the day I called in sick. Or maybe not."

"But why wouldn't you take it seriously, Jenn? You were pregnant."

My heart began to race with anxiety. "I don't know. I just wasn't thinking clearly, I guess. My brain feels like cotton lately."

"Have there been any other instances where you've felt that way? Or have there been missing blocks of time?"

I thought about an afternoon the previous week when I noticed a bad smell in the car. Eventually I found three grocery bags in the trunk but had no idea how they'd gotten there. The meat was rancid and the milk was curdled in the summer heat, so they'd been sitting there awhile.

Like so many other inexplicable events lately, I'd blamed it on a severe case of "pregnancy brain." Or maybe Sylvie had put the bags there.

"Yes," I replied.

Just then, my laptop chimed. Darting a concerned glance at the clock, I said, "It's Jake, but he's not supposed to call until midnight."

My stomach exploded with dread. I met Sylvie's eyes.

"Do you want me to talk to him for you?" she asked.

"No, I need to do it. Can you leave us alone please? And turn the light on for me?"

She nodded, rose to her feet and flicked the light switch on at the door before closing it behind her.

With a deep, nervous breath, I raised the screen of my laptop.

"Hey, babe," I said, forcing a smile. "You're early."

❦

There was panic in Jake's eyes and I knew immediately that something was wrong.

"I'm sorry, Jenn," he said, "I can't talk for too long. I have to go in about sixty seconds. I shouldn't even have called but I wanted to find out how it went today."

I sat forward. "What do you mean, you have to go? It sounds urgent."

"It's no big deal," he replied.

Of course, I knew he was lying. My blood quickened. "Are you going to be okay?"

"We'll be fine. It's just a routine mission, but we might be gone a few days. Maybe even a week. I won't be able to get in touch with you, but I don't want you to worry about anything."

"Will it be dangerous?" I asked, reaching forward to touch the screen with the tips of my fingers.

He glanced over his shoulder as if to check for anyone listening in on our conversation. For a brief, fretful moment I thought he might confide in me, but when he faced the camera again, he said, "Not dangerous at all. I just wanted to hear your voice before I left."

A ball of heat rolled over in my belly. I had to fight hard not to give in to the worst kinds of forebodings.

"I'm so glad you called," I said.

"How did it go today?" He glanced over his shoulder again, preoccupied and impatient. I knew we didn't have much time.

"Great," I heard myself saying, feeling rather hazy about what he was asking and what the correct answer was. "It went really well."

"I wish I could have been there," he replied.

"Me, too."

"I'm sorry baby," he continued. "I know this is rushed, but you have to tell me. I want to know before we take off so I can give the guys the news. Boy or girl?"

I blinked a few times. My connection to him seemed to hang on a thread. *Would I lose him? Where was he going?*

"Jenn?" he prodded and I knew I had to answer his question. "Boy or girl?"

Lord help me. The words spilled out of my mouth before I could stop them. "It's a girl."

Joy spread across Jake's face. He let out a tearful laugh. "A girl? No kidding? That's amazing!" His eyes glistened. "How are *you* doing? Are you okay?"

"Of course. I'm fine. Really, everything's wonderful. Don't worry."

But I wasn't fine. I'd lost our child. And something strange was happening to me—something I didn't understand.

"I'm so happy, Jenn," he replied. "I can't wait to get home to you."

"Me, too." Again, I reached out and touched the screen.

He nodded and glanced over his shoulder. "I really have to go." Leaning forward, he kissed the camera. "Bye, hon. I love you."

Like a flick of a switch, he was gone.

I sat there in stunned silence, unable to move. *This isn't happening.*

A knock sounded at my door.

How long had I been sitting there just staring at the blank computer screen? I had no idea.

Sylvie entered. Her hand came to rest gently on my shoulder. "Are you okay?"

I looked up at her in a daze. "He's going away. I think it's going to be dangerous. He asked about the baby and I didn't know how to answer."

"What did you say?" Sylvie asked with concern.

I gazed up at her pleadingly, as if she could absolve me somehow for the lie I'd just told my husband.

"If he's distracted," I explained, "even for a second, he could get killed. I don't want him to have bad thoughts in his head. I don't want him to be upset—and if the worst happens…You know, if he…" *Oh, God, I couldn't say it.* "If the worst happens, he needs to believe he's leaving something good behind. He needs to know I'm okay."

"You didn't tell him…" Sylvie said with disbelief.

Still floating in a mindless stupor of dread and confusion, I shook my head.

"What did you say to him, Jenn?" she firmly asked. "*Tell* me."

Panic swarmed into my belly. "God help me, Sylvie. I told him it was a girl. What am I going to do? Please help me. Tell me what to do."

She sank down on the edge of the bed and covered her face with her hands.

❧

November 9

I woke up feeling knifelike stabs of guilt, grief, and fear. At first I didn't understand where they were coming from. Then I remembered: The guilt was from lying to my husband; the grief was from the loss of my child; and the fear was for the future—both Jake's and my own.

Where was he? Would he be safe? What would he do when he found out I'd lied to him? As for my own situation, and why I couldn't remember my miscarriage...*Was I losing my mind?*

"I'm taking you straight to the ER," Mom said as she set a plate of scrambled eggs and toast in front of me.

I looked down at it without interest. I couldn't even bring myself to pick up my fork. "I'll call my regular doctor today and make an appointment."

"What if she can't see you?" Mom challenged. "I think we should just go to the hospital. This is serious, Jenn."

"It's not an emergency."

"Yes, it is. Do you even hear yourself?"

For some reason in that moment, no matter what she said, I simply couldn't grasp the fact that something was wrong with me. Maybe some part of me knew there was, but another part was in denial. Of course I was upset. I'd just learned I'd had a miscarriage. We just had to stay calm.

Suddenly I became aware of Sylvie standing at the counter refilling her coffee cup. "Why aren't you at school?" I asked.

"I thought I should stay home today," she replied, looking at me disapprovingly, as if I were a criminal.

"Why?"

She raised an eyebrow. "Really, Jenn? You have to ask why?"

Blankly, I stared down at my breakfast.

"It's not going to eat itself," Mom said, taking a seat across from me at the table.

"I'm not hungry," I replied.

My mother's shoulders slumped with disappointment. "You have to eat, darling."

"I will," I replied. "Just not right now. I don't feel so good. I want to go back to bed."

Mom and Sylvie exchanged looks of concern, so I pushed my chair back and stood. I froze, however, when a soft buzzing sound began in my head. I couldn't seem to make my body work. I couldn't even put one foot in front of the other.

"What is that smell?" I asked my mother. "Is it lemons?"

"I don't smell anything," she replied.

A shiver of anxiety moved through me, followed by intense heart palpitations. I sat back down on the chair.

"Are you all right?" Sylvie asked.

"I feel strange."

For a long moment I sat and stared at my open palms. All my extremities grew cold and numb. I wanted to ask what was going on, but I couldn't seem to remember what words I wanted to say, or how to put them in the right order to make a sentence.

Then pins and needles spread over my skin from the soles of my bare feet to the top of my head. All my muscles tensed up, hard as steel. I wanted to scream but I couldn't.

The next thing I knew, everything was fading to white and I was vaguely aware of falling sideways out of my chair.

When I came to, I was lying on my side, wildly disoriented with a killer headache. I didn't know where I was or how much time had elapsed since I fell out of my chair in the kitchen. My tongue was sore. I tasted something metallic. Was it blood?

Where was I? What was happening?

Growing increasingly panicked and agitated, I blinked a few times and tried to focus on my surroundings. I still couldn't seem to move my body.

There was a blue curtain…

The room was brightly lit…

I couldn't make sense of any of these things, however. I realized I was drooling.

Then my mother's face came into view. "Jenn, can you hear me?"

Huh? I was comforted by the sight of her, yet I couldn't comprehend her words, nor could I form a reply.

I felt very depressed and my muscles hurt.

"You're okay," she said. "You're in the ER."

I couldn't figure out why I was in Emergency. Nothing made sense to me.

"You had a seizure," she added.

I became aware of people talking to me and asking questions. They were strangers. "Hi Jenn. Can you tell me your name?"

I couldn't.

"Do you know what day it is?"

All I could do was mumble, "Huh?"

"You're all right," someone else said to me, "but you hit your head when you fell."

"We had to call an ambulance," my mother told me.

"We're going to do some tests," I heard. "How are you feeling? Can you say your name?"

I was only vaguely aware of what these words meant or where I was. My eyes fell closed and I drifted off to sleep.

The next time I woke, I was lying on my back in a hospital bed, hooked up to oxygen. I was too weak to move, but I was able to turn my head to the side and look at a blue curtain. I heard other people talking and I knew I was in a hospital ward with other patients.

Again, my mother's face came into view. "Hi sweetie," she gently said as she rubbed my cheek. "It's nice to have you back."

The headache had diminished, but I was still groggy and weak. "What happened?"

"You had a seizure this morning," she explained. "By the time the paramedics arrived the seizure was over but you wouldn't wake up and your head was bleeding so they took you the hospital. Then you had another seizure in the ambulance. They gave you some sort of IV drug that made it stop."

I wet my lips. "My tongue hurts."

"You bit it when you were seizing."

"Where's Sylvie?" I asked.

"She just went to the cafeteria to get something to eat. She'll be back soon."

I lay quietly for a moment, struggling to understand all this. "How long was I asleep?" I asked.

"About six hours."

Still extremely fatigued, I closed my eyes again. I must have drifted off because I woke to the sound of Sylvie's voice.

"Jenn, the doctor's here. Can you answer some questions?"

I opened my eyes to discover a handsome male physician, possibly about forty years old, standing over my bed. "Hi Jenn. I'm Dr. Samson and I'm a neurologist. How are you feeling?"

"Tired," I replied. "Mom said I had a seizure."

"That's right. Two of them, actually. Do you remember any of that?"

"Not much." I wanted to give him as much information as I could, but I had to speak slowly. "Just a weird buzzing in my head before it started. It felt like my brain was twitching."

"What else do you remember?"

I blinked my eyes and focused on the ceiling. "I was anxious and couldn't talk or make my body move. Then all my muscles started to tense up and I fell off the chair. I don't remember anything after that."

He nodded and wrote something down on my chart. "While you were sleeping this afternoon, your sister and mother were able to tell me a few things about your medical history and the fact that you had a miscarriage recently?"

I swallowed and nodded my head.

"Sylvie also told me you've possibly been suffering from some memory loss and personality changes—that sometimes you can't think clearly. Or you say or do inappropriate things. Can you tell me how long that's been going on?"

Continuing to blink up at the ceiling I struggled to remember when it all began. "It's difficult to know. I was pregnant so I thought that's what was causing it. I guess about a month or two."

I described things like leaving groceries in my car and possibly smashing my honeymoon picture, but having no memory of it. Judging by the doctor's lack of a reaction, I suspected Sylvie had already told him about that.

"Was today the first time you've had a seizure?" he asked.

"Yes."

He wrote something else down and I looked at my mother. She moved quickly to my side and squeezed my hand.

"What's wrong with me?" I asked. "Do you know?"

At last, the doctor stopped writing and lowered the chart to his side. "Yes. After you came in, we put you on a Dilantin drip to prevent any more seizures, and we were able to do some tests. We also did a full round of blood work and a CT scan."

"I didn't wake up for that?"

He shook his head. "No. You had what we call post-ictal fatigue. It's common for patients to sleep very deeply after a seizure."

I glanced at my mother again. She was looking at me with great compassion while Sylvie stood at the foot of my bed, staring at me with concern.

"Do you have the results of the CT scan?" I asked with growing unease.

The doctor regarded me intently and paused as if to give me a few seconds to brace myself. "You have a tumor on your brain, Jenn. It's pressing on both your frontal and temporal lobes."

Stark white terror shot into my core. Had I heard him correctly?

I glanced at my mother again. She squeezed my hand tighter.

"Am I going to die?" I asked.

"Not if we can help it," Dr. Samson replied.

"Everything will be fine," Sylvie promised.

I had a hard time believing her, however, because nothing had been fine in my life lately. All the worst possible things that could ever happen to a person seemed to be happening to me all at once. *What next, God? What do you have in store for me next?*

"Is this why I lost my baby?" I asked Dr. Samson.

He spoke matter-of-factly. "The two events were most likely unrelated, though it's impossible to know for sure. Your sister mentioned you don't remember having your miscarriage?"

"That's right."

Dr. Samson paused. "I'm sorry to hear about that, Jenn, but at least this explains why you might not remember. The pressure on your frontal lobe can cause all sorts of things—loss of memory, changes in personality and behavior, loss of inhibitions, confusion, distraction...."

"What can we do?" I asked. "Is it possible to treat it?"

"Yes. We're recommending surgery."

"*Brain* surgery?" I exclaimed. "You can't fix it with radiation or something?"

He shook his head. "The neurosurgeon will be in here to see you later. His name is Dr. Phillips and he'll be able to answer any specific questions you might have about the procedure, but for now I can tell you that surgery to remove it is your best option. Let me assure you that Dr. Phillips is highly skilled. He's done hundreds of procedures just like this. You'll be in excellent hands."

I lay there for a moment, letting all this sink in. "I can't believe it. When would it happen?" I asked the doctor.

"Tomorrow or the day after."

What? The breath sailed out of my lungs. I felt an instinctive urge to sit up on the bed, rip the IV out of my hand and run straight out of there.

"That soon?" I asked. "No…that's not possible. I have to talk to my husband first."

"I understand he's in Afghanistan," the doctor mentioned, consulting my chart.

"Yes, and I can't get in touch with him right now. He's away on a mission and said he might be gone for a week. What if something happens to me during the operation? I can't do this without him knowing."

And I have to tell him about the miscarriage…

"Can't we wait a week?" I pleaded. "Would there be any additional risks to putting it off for that long?"

"Yes, there would be some risks," Dr. Samson replied, "but we could put it off for a week. No longer than that, though. It's a mid-sized tumor, but that could change. These things are unpredictable. I wouldn't want it to become inoperable. And there's the danger of seizures as well." He gestured toward the bandage on my head. "You know what can happen if you fall. You were lucky this time, but you could have broken something."

"I could stay home from work," I offered. "I'd be really careful. And lots of people live with seizures, don't they? People with epilepsy…"

He consulted my chart. "We've had you on a Dilantin drip since you came in this morning. As a compromise, I'd like to keep you overnight for observation just to make sure you're responding well to the medication. If I see no problems with that, I can give you pills to take during the week to prevent any more seizures. And I'd want you to come in mid-week for a check-up."

"That sounds fine," I said. "It would give me time to contact my husband's commander and let him know what's happening. Maybe they can fly him home."

Please, let that be an option…

To my surprise and relief, the doctor agreed. I would be discharged the following day and my surgery would be scheduled for six days later.

S till fatigued from my seizure, I napped a lot in the hospital. Sylvie went to school because she was nearing mid-term exams and couldn't afford to miss any additional time. It was my mother who stayed at my bedside, fetching me water, making cheerful conversation about the latest reality shows, and showing me pictures out of the gossip magazines.

I must have been asleep when Sylvie arrived late in the afternoon because I woke to the sound of her and my mother speaking in quiet tones.

"Are you sure that's a good idea?" my mother whispered.

"Why wouldn't it be?" Sylvie replied.

I opened my eyes but didn't move on the bed. I was able to watch my mother angrily turn the pages of her magazine. "You've come so far, Sylvie. Why stir the pot?"

"Because it needs to be stirred, Mom. I think it helps me."

"How could it help you? I think you just enjoy torturing yourself, going to the nursery to look at those babies. After what happened to your sister…Losing her child and now this…Why do we even have to go there?"

"You mean emotionally?" Sylvie asked. "Dr. Ramone says it's good for me to face my emotions and deal with them head on."

My mother let out an angry huff. "Just keep it to yourself, all right? Jenn's been through enough. She doesn't need to hear about how cute they are."

I closed my eyes and decided not to involve myself in their argument because my mother was right. I didn't want to hear how cute all those newborn babies were. I was still grieving the loss of my own.

November 12

"Don't worry," I said to Sylvie over dinner the night before my mid-week checkup. "I'll be fine."

I'd been doing well since my discharge from the hospital and had experienced no seizures or memory lapses. The Dilantin was working like a dream.

My mother had traveled home the day before to tend to her dog, Chocolate, a six-year-old Shih Tzu she'd adopted after my father passed away. A neighbor had been taking care of Chocolate, but Mom needed to make other arrangements before returning for my surgery—and staying indefinitely afterward—which she fully intended to do.

"I'll take a cab to the hospital and back," I promised Sylvie, "and you can text me every hour, but I'm not letting you miss your exam."

She pushed her salad around on her plate with a fork. "What time do you have to be there?"

"At 7:00 a.m. for blood work," I replied. "Then I have to hang around until 12:00 to see Dr. Samson for the results and then there's my checkup. I'll bring a book and go to the cafeteria. What could possibly happen? If I pass out or seize—*which I won't*—at least I'll be in a hospital."

Thankfully my sister didn't argue. "Fine," she said, "but promise to text me every hour, except while I'm writing my exam between 11:00 and 1:00."

"I will."

"And be sure to bring your phone charger."

I laughed. "Good Lord! Everything will be fine and I won't forget. I promise."

"Good."

We finished our supper. A few minutes later, just as we were rising to clean off the table, my laptop chimed from the bedroom.

I froze in my spot. "Do you think it's Jake? Maybe he's coming home."

My sister met my alarmed gaze. "Well, don't just stand there. Go answer it and find out."

I set my plate down on the counter and rushed out of the kitchen.

—ꝰ—

"Baby..." Jake said.

I was never so happy to see my husband's handsome face. Those thoughtful, loving eyes. Thank God he was all right.

"What's going on?" he asked. Then he shocked me by bowing his head into the crook of his elbow and choking back a low, tortured sob. I'd never seen him weep before, not like that, and a hot tear rolled down my cheek.

"I guess they must have told you," I said. *But how much did he know?*

He leaned forward and met my eyes. "They said you have a brain tumor. I didn't believe it. Tell me it's not true. It can't be."

Dear God...

I reached out and touched the screen. "I'm so sorry, Jake."

His eyes were bloodshot and glassy. "How could this happen? *Why?*"

Swallowing uneasily, I shook my head because I didn't have those answers. I'd been asking the same questions myself. "Bad luck, I guess."

He wiped a tear from his cheek. "How did you find out? Were you having headaches?"

I explained how it progressed from headaches and a few inconvenient episodes of forgetfulness to a full-blown seizure in my kitchen, and how Sylvie and my mother had called an ambulance and taken me to the ER.

Suddenly, Jake stood up. He knocked his chair over and disappeared from sight.

"Jake!" I shouted, leaning forward. For a moment I watched the blank wall in the background while I listened to the sounds of him pacing around.

Please come back.

At last he reappeared on the screen, picked up his chair and sat down again. He was breathing heavily and his face was flushed.

"You're angry," I said.

"Yes. I can't believe this is happening to you. That I wasn't there to be with you, to take care of you."

"I'm fine," I assured him. "I have good support here with Sylvie and Mom. You don't have to worry about that part."

He looked away. I saw a vein pulsing at his temple and knew he was fighting hard to manage his frustration. "They said you're having surgery on Thursday?"

"That's right," I replied. "Can you come home for that?"

He nodded and I let out a breath of relief. "Thank goodness."

"They're flying me out in an hour," he explained. "With the time change and connections, I should be home by tomorrow night. I'll call you on your cell when I know more."

I felt suddenly weightless and very blessed. *My husband was coming home.* "I'll be so happy to see you," I said.

"Me, too." He touched the screen. "I love you, babe."

"I love you, too. Fly safe."

He kissed the camera lens and the screen went blank. Leaning forward over the keyboard, I cradled my head in my arms. Deeply and slowly I breathed in and out.

Jake...

I'd always been an optimist, but rarely had I felt more hopeful and happy than I did in that moment. Joy bubbled up within me and I found myself laughing and crying at the same time.

How miraculous. Even with a tumor on my brain, I still believed the future was bright. There was so much to look forward to because my husband was alive; he loved me and he was coming home to support me.

Wiping the tears from my eyes with the backs of my hand, I decided with certainty that come hell or high water, I was going to make it through the surgery. I began to visualize myself in the recovery room afterward.

The doctors will tell me I have a clean bill of health. Jake and I will both weep tears of joy. We'll try again to have another baby. It'll be a girl...Later, I'll watch her play in a sandbox in the backyard. She'll be three years old by then. We'll have a puppy and I'll be pregnant again...

Rising from my chair, I turned and jumped at the sight of my sister standing behind me. Laying a hand over my pounding heart, I said, "I didn't hear you come in."

"I apologize," she replied. "I couldn't help it. I wanted to know if he'd be able to come home."

"He's on his way," I told her as I brushed past to finish tidying up in the kitchen. "He'll be home in time for the surgery."

"Did you tell him about the baby?" she asked.

I stopped and glanced over my shoulder. "Not yet."

She didn't say a word, but I felt her disapproval like a cold outdoor breeze at my back. Maybe I should have said something, but I walked out because I didn't want anything to spoil my mood.

The following morning I rose early for my appointment at the hospital, took a long hot shower, called a cab, and left the house while Sylvie was still sleeping soundly.

The cab dropped me off at the main entrance shortly before 7:00 a.m. I went straight to the blood drawing clinic where I only had to wait a few minutes before someone called my name.

Sylvie

November 13

As luck would have it, I slept late the morning of my midterm, which meant I didn't have time to shower or eat breakfast. I rushed out the door in a panic and was lucky not to get pulled over for speeding as I raced across town.

As soon as I found a parking spot and spilled out of my car in a tangle of limbs and books, I dug into my purse for my phone and texted Jenn.

By this time it was 10:50 a.m.

I slept in. How are you doing?

She immediately texted me back. *I'm doing great.*

Good. Heading into my exam now. I'll text you later.

Good luck, she replied.

Since my instructor was strict about cell phones in class, especially during exams, I shut off my phone and slipped it back into my purse.

I suppose, under the circumstances, I should explain why I'd slept in that morning and didn't text Jenn when I said I would.

The truth is, I'd tossed and turned all night long, wondering if I should have called Jake myself and told him about Jenn's miscarriage.

Or forced her to do it herself.

Fine. I'll admit it. I was eavesdropping on their conversation on the laptop again the night before, but the fact of the matter was this: She hadn't said a word about the baby when she'd spoken to him and I was certain it was only going to make things more difficult when he arrived home. I doubted he would be quite so sympathetic when he found out she'd kept something like that from him. *Twice.*

I wasn't sure if it was intentional on her part. Maybe she'd made a conscious decision not to drop another bomb on him last night when he was so distraught about the tumor. I knew how sensitive she was to his fears about losing another child. Maybe she wanted to tell him in person.

Or maybe she'd simply forgotten to tell him—which wasn't out of the question, considering her condition.

And so...Last night I hadn't slept. This was not unusual for me because I had a tendency to stress out about things I'd said or didn't say. It always hit me hardest during the night. I would replay conversations over and over in my mind, analyze them to death, and wish I'd handled them differently.

My anxiety medications were helpful, but still, in extreme circumstances like these, I tortured myself by worrying about the future and the past. I had to physically restrain myself from calling my mother or therapist at 3:00 a.m. to ask for advice. What would *they* think? Would they advise me to call Jake immediately and break the news to him myself? Maybe Jenn needed my help to do that.

Or maybe that would be meddling. Would I be butting my nose in where it didn't belong?

Anyway, that's why I'd slept in—because I'd tossed and turned from midnight until dawn. It's also why I was so distracted during my exam and for the rest of the day when I couldn't stop debating with myself about what to do.

In the end, I called my mother after the exam and discussed it with her. She told me to butt out.

Then I called my therapist and she was able to squeeze me in for a quick fifteen-minute phone call. She also told me it wasn't my responsibility. It was Jenn's marriage. It was between the two of *them*. She coached me into trusting Jenn—despite her brain tumor—to know what was best and to let the cards fall where they may.

I'm still not sure it was the right decision, but I decided not to interfere. At least not while Jake was still in the sky.

I immediately knew that something was wrong when I pulled into the driveway. There were no lights on inside the house. This came as a surprise to me because I'd texted Jenn more than a few times throughout the day to check on her, and each time she replied that she was fine. The last message said she was lying down to take a nap, so maybe she was still sleeping.

It was not until I turned on the lights in the kitchen and listened to the message on the answering machine that I allowed myself to take a flying leap right into the deep end of the anxiety pool. I finished listening to the message, searched the house, and immediately dialed 9-1-1.

"It took you long enough to get here," I said to the uniformed police officer when he finally arrived and rang the doorbell. "Come in, come in."

He entered the house and I nearly stumbled backwards because he was a large, strapping man.

"I'm Officer Jenkins," he said. "Somebody called about a missing person?"

"Yes, it's my sister. The dispatcher said you don't normally consider a person missing until twenty-four hours, but this is a special case. My sister has a brain tumor and sometimes she gets confused or can't remember things."

He pulled out his notepad. "What's her name?"

"Jennifer Nichols, but she goes by Jenn. She's having an operation in a few days to remove the tumor, and she had an appointment at the hospital for blood work and a checkup today. She showed up for the blood work at 7:00 a.m., but she didn't show up for her appointment with the doctor at noon. She was supposed to stay in the hospital and just read a book or something."

"When was the last time you spoke with her?" he asked.

This was the part I knew would get dicey. "Umm...we've been texting each other throughout the day. She was replying to everything until about three hours ago. She said she was lying down to take a nap. I haven't heard from her since."

With his pen poised over the notepad, he paused. It took a few seconds for his eyes to lift and meet mine. "So it's only been three hours? And you just got home? Maybe she woke up, went out shopping and her phone died."

I let out a frustrated breath. "My sister's not a shopper. But that's not the point. The point is that she missed her appointment at the hospital and she's not here. She's not allowed to drive because she might have a seizure. Oh, God, what if she did go the mall and had a seizure?"

"I thought you said she wasn't a shopper."

"She isn't," I corrected. "Just...hypothetically."

He regarded me with skepticism. "I'm sure you would have heard something if she had a seizure in a public place. Someone would have called an ambulance and if she was taken to a hospital, they would have contacted a family member."

I waved my hands in front of my face and paced around the kitchen. "No, no, that's not what happened."

"What did happen, exactly?" he asked with a note of impatience, as if I were some sort of anxiety-ridden, PMS female on medication—which I totally was, except for the PMS—but I knew I wasn't wrong about this.

"I came home to a phone message from the hospital," I tried to explain in a calm voice. "It said that she missed her appointment at noon, and that if she wanted to reschedule, she had to call back. But there's no good reason why she would miss that appointment. And if she didn't go to it, why didn't she at least tell me that and come home?"

He checked his watch. "Maybe she did but went out again for a bite to eat?"

I felt my heart begin to race. "Pardon me, Officer Jenkins. You're not *listening* to me. My sister has a brain tumor and she can get confused sometimes or become forgetful. She might have wandered off somewhere. She might be having a seizure at this very moment."

Was I overreacting? Maybe I was. I needed to lower my voice and talk slower. Maybe that's why he wasn't taking me seriously.

Officer Jenkins closed his notepad. "Do you have a picture of her?"

"Yes." I moved quickly into the living room to the photo albums on the bookshelf, pulled out the most recent one, flipped through it and slid out a 4x5. "Here she is. Jenn Nichols. Last seen at the hospital for blood work at 7:00 a.m. This was taken last summer. Her hair's the same now."

"What would she be wearing?"

"A red winter coat with a hood. Probably jeans. I didn't see her leave this morning, but she usually wears jeans."

He took a good look at the picture and slipped it into his pocket. "Would you mind if I had a look at your cell phone texts?"

"Of course." Pleased that he was at least taking an interest, I rifled through my purse for my phone, found her messages and handed it to him.

He wrote down the times of her replies and the exact wording, but there wasn't much to go on. The texts were all brief and to the point: *I'm fine…I'm doing great…Everything's good…I'm tired. I need to take a nap.*

"Did you have a good look around the house when you got home?" he asked. "Was anything out of order?"

"What do you mean?"

His eyes scanned the living room. "Is anything missing? A suitcase, maybe? Is she married? Is there a boyfriend? Was there any sign of a struggle?"

"No, nothing like that," I replied. "She's happily married and her husband Jake is in Afghanistan…or he *was.* He's on his way home today. He should arrive any time."

"Have you contacted him yet?"

"I tried calling him but his cell phone is turned off. He's probably still in the air."

Officer Jenkins returned to the kitchen. "Mind if I take a look around?"

"Be my guest." I followed him down the hall to Jenn's room. He wandered in, scanned the room with his eyes, then moved out into the hall.

"This your room?" he asked, opening the door to enter.

"Yes. I um…didn't have time to make my bed this morning." I quickly picked my pajamas up off the floor and threw them into the hamper.

Next, he peered into the bathroom, then walked to the spare room. "What's in here?"

"Jenn uses it for storage—mostly Jake's stuff since I moved in here. He was supposed to be gone for nine months."

Jenkins opened the door and walked in. I followed, turned on the light, and lost my breath.

"Is there a child living here?" Jenkins asked.

I gazed around with wide eyes. All my stuff and Jake's was piled high in boxes against the far wall to clear space for a crib and change table under the window. The curtains had been changed. They were now pink. "This is weird."

"Why?" he asked.

"Because my sister had a miscarriage recently. Before that, this was earmarked to be the baby's room, but she hadn't gotten around to fixing it up. She wanted to wait until after she knew if it was going to be a boy or a girl. Then she lost the baby."

"Looks like she's expecting a girl," he said, opening the closet to find pink and white baby clothes hung up or folded on the shelves.

I moved deeper into the room to look at everything. "I'm not sure when she did this, but it must have been this week."

"How do you know?"

"Because there was nothing done in here when she had her seizure and found out about the tumor. I know because I came in to get some stuff that morning, just before it happened. She certainly didn't have a crib set up."

"When did she lose the baby?" he asked.

"We're not positive, exactly. She can't remember. Memory loss is a symptom of the tumor," I tried to explain.

He nodded. "Anything else out of order?"

"I don't know. Let's take a look in the basement."

We checked that out but nothing struck me as unusual.

"What about the husband?" Officer Jenkins asked as we climbed back up the stairs. "When did you say he'd be back?"

"Any time now. He said he'd call her when his flight landed, but I've been texting her and she won't answer." I followed the detective back to the kitchen.

"Listen, you seem like a nice lady," Jenkins said, handing me a card, "so I'm going to file a report, but call this number right away if your sister comes home or if the husband shows up."

"What do you think's going on?" I asked as I read the information on the card.

He shrugged casually. "You said the husband's coming home from Afghanistan today. They might just be in a hotel somewhere. Who could blame them?"

I stared at him in disbelief. "No, she would have called me, or at least she would have answered my texts. She would have shown up for her appointment. Can't you put a trace on her phone or something?"

He nodded at me condescendingly. "You said the husband's not answering his cell either. Maybe they're both just a little preoccupied." With that he walked out.

I watched Jenkins saunter down the driveway to his squad car, then I kicked the door shut behind him.

Five minutes later—after deciding to take matters into my own hands—I got into my car, backed out of the driveway and drove to the hospital to search for her. With any luck, she'd be sitting in a waiting room somewhere, reading her book or taking a nap.

Riley

CHAPTER

Thirty-seven

⸎

November 14

When my mother, my sister Holly and her husband Josh found me at the baggage carousel at the airport, I nearly fell to my knees in gratitude at the sight of them.

"Thanks for coming," I said to my mom as I wrapped my arms around her and held her as tightly as I could without crushing her. Holly joined us as well.

Moments later, after I pulled myself together, I shook hands with Josh, the childhood friend I'd known since I was three years old. "I hope it wasn't a problem getting some time off work."

"Not a problem at all," he replied. "I guess my lieutenant still feels like he owes me something. Works out well for me sometimes."

It always surprised me that my brother-in-law could speak so lightly about the fact that he'd been shot twice in the line of duty two years ago while pursuing an armed suspect through the streets of Boston. He'd nearly died on the operating table and had been in a coma for five days.

Damn right the police department owed him.

In that moment, I spotted a young woman on the opposite side of the carousel with a baby in a chest carrier and a diaper bag slung over her shoulder. She was greeting an older couple, most likely her parents or in-laws. I wondered if she knew how lucky she was to have her child so close and safe in her arms.

Clearing my throat, I turned my eyes away from them and helped my mother with her bag. Josh took Holly's hand and they followed me outside to where my car was parked and waiting.

"I'm sure they did a thorough search of your house," Josh said as we pulled into my driveway, "but I can take a look around if you want me to. You never know. Maybe they missed something."

"That would be great." I shut off the engine, got out and fetched Mom's bag out of the trunk.

Holly and Josh wheeled their own suitcases inside where we met Carol at the door. "Flight was on time?" she asked, inviting everyone in.

I stepped aside to allow my family to enter first, then proceeded with the introductions. "Everyone, this is Carol, Lois's mother. Carol, this is my mother Margie, my sister Holly and her husband Josh."

"You're the police officer," Carol said as she shook his hand. "You'll be handy to have around, that's for sure."

"I hope I can help," he replied.

Trudy—wearing her red and white polka-dot pajamas and dragging her doll Polly along the floor—appeared in the doorway from the living room. I heard the sound of a cartoon on television.

"I hope you don't mind," Carol whispered to me. "I told them they could stay up until you got home."

"That's fine," I replied, bending to scoop Trudy up into my arms. "Look who's here." I turned to face my family.

She held out her arms. "Grammy…"

"Hi, sweetheart." My mother hugged Trudy and kissed her on the cheek. "I'm so happy to see you. I brought you a present. It's in my suitcase."

Danny came out to greet them as well and there were hugs and kisses all around.

Carol took everyone's coats and hung them in the closet. "I'm staying in the spare bedroom," she said, "but I set up an inflatable mattress in Danny's room for Trudy, so you can have her room, Margie. Holly and Josh, I made up some beds for you in the rec room downstairs. If you'd like to go settle in, I can heat up some soup for you on the stove. Are you hungry?"

"Soup would be lovely, thank you," Holly replied.

Everyone went their separate ways to unpack, which left me standing in the doorway to the living room, watching my two children lounge about on the sofa, immersed in one of the *Toy Story* DVDs.

Everything seemed so normal within these four walls. The comforting sound of the cartoon, my children safe and cozy in their pajamas. But nothing was normal. Not here in this house, or outside in the world.

Naturally, I was grateful for the presence of my family, but I was still nauseous over the fact that my newborn child had been stolen from me.

Where are you, baby girl? Can you hear me? Do you know how much we love you?

After serving bowls of hot chicken soup for all of us at the table, Carol returned to the hospital to be with Lois. Deciding I was in no hurry to put Danny and Trudy to bed, I turned a blind eye when the credits rolled on their movie and Danny discreetly got up and slid the sequel into the DVD player.

"Was she able to give you a detailed description of the woman?" Josh asked, leaning back in his chair to glance over his shoulder at Trudy who was lying sleepily on her side on the sofa, sucking her thumb and hugging her doll. "Did they attempt to use a sketch artist?"

"No," I replied. "She was too vague about the woman's facial features. She said they were foggy, or hazy."

Holly's head drew back in confusion. "She doesn't wear glasses, does she?"

"No, I'm not sure what she meant by that. I guess it was dark in the room. One thing she was certain about, though, was the long, wavy, brown hair pulled back in a ponytail and the tattoo on the woman's forearm. Right here." I rolled up my sleeve and rubbed a finger over the inside of my wrist. "That's all we have to go on, really."

Knowing what Lois would think of me allowing the children to stay up this late on a school night, I called out to Danny. "Hey there, sneaky. I saw you put that movie in just now. If you think you're staying up until midnight to finish it, you're dreaming."

"I know," he replied with a smile.

We all chuckled softly from the kitchen.

Trudy yawned, rolled onto her back, then slid off the sofa to join us. "I'm tired," she mumbled as she climbed onto my lap.

I kissed the top of her head. "No wonder. It's way past your bedtime."

"I don't want to sleep in Danny's room," she said. "Can I sleep with you, Grammy?"

I met my mother's gaze questioningly.

"Of course you can," she cheerfully replied. "I'd love that. We can snuggle all night."

Holly's cell phone—which was lying on the table in front of her—vibrated and rang with a familiar ring tone, the main theme from *Star Wars*. Trudy giggled and leaned forward to look at it.

"It's the lady," she said, smiling.

Holly picked up her phone and checked the call display. Her eyes met mine. "It's Dad."

My father. Rarely did he ever call *me* on my cell phone. Not that I expected him to, or wanted it. At least we'd made it over the hurdle of learning how to speak to each other again—as men. He had grandchildren now and my mother insisted. Though I knew we would never be close, at least we were civil with each other, which was all I could ask for. We both had our regrets. We'd both made our mistakes. On some level, we both understood that and were able to bury the hatchet. Though it would always, for the rest of my days, be in a shallow grave.

Holly swiped the screen. "Hello? Hi, Dad. Yes, we made it. Flight was on time." She paused. "No, still no news. Yes, Lois is doing fine. Riley says she was moved out of the ICU this afternoon."

Trudy turned on my lap and cupped my face in her tiny hands, squeezed my cheeks hard until I puckered my lips like a fish. "It's the lady," she said again.

"No, it's Grampy," I replied.

"Do you want to say hi to him?" Holly asked Trudy, holding out the phone to her.

Trudy rested her small ear against it. "Hello? Hi, Grampy. I love you, too. I know it's late…" Long pause. "He's watching *Toy Story*. I'm going to sleep with Grammy tonight." Another long pause. "Yes…No." She giggled. "Okay. Bye."

Holly took the phone and briefly continued her conversation with our father. Then she ended the call and set the phone down on the table. "He said he wishes he could be here, but he has two surgeries tomorrow that can't be postponed."

"I understand," I replied, struggling to hold onto Trudy who was squirming like an octopus on my lap, reaching for Holly's phone.

Eventually, Holly laughed, picked it up and handed it to her. "Do you want to play with it?"

Trudy took hold of it and pressed the home button. "It's the lady."

Something in my stomach lurched, which sent a flood of adrenaline into my veins. "What lady?"

Trudy pointed at the screensaver on Holly's phone. "The lady with the numbers on her arm."

I grabbed the phone out of my daughter's hands. There, staring back at me, was a photo of my sister Leah, who had passed away two years ago.

❝A re you sure this is her?" I asked Trudy, pointing at the digital photograph. My eyes met Holly's. "When was this taken?"

"About four years ago," she replied, "when she was first diagnosed. We went to the beach that day."

I squinted to try and focus on Leah's arm and used the tips of my fingers to enlarge the photo. "Did she have a tattoo?"

"No way," Holly replied. "She hated tattoos."

Trudy pointed again. "That's the lady."

I looked across the table at my mother, who was staring at me, openmouthed. My shock and confusion reflected back at me through her eyes.

"Maybe Leah has a look-alike out there somewhere," Mom suggested, appearing visibly shaken by the notion.

No, that couldn't be…"If I told you this lady's name," I said to Trudy, "would you recognize it? Was it Leah?"

Trudy shrugged her shoulders.

"She doesn't know," Holly said, reaching for her phone. "But I have other pictures saved on here." She opened her gallery, scrolled through, found something and showed it to Trudy. "Is this her?"

Trudy looked at it and nodded.

Holly scrolled through and found another. "What about this one?"

Trudy nodded again.

"And this?" Again, she nodded her head, then wrapped her arms around my neck.

"I'm tired, Daddy."

"Okay, honey. I'll take you to bed."

My mother rose to her feet and held out her arms. "Let me take her, Riley, since we're sharing a room."

As I handed my daughter to my mother, Josh said, "Wait a second, Margie, before you take her. Riley, do you have a piece of paper and a black pen? Like a Sharpie or something?"

I rose and tore a sheet off the notepad by the refrigerator, then handed it to Josh along with a black pen.

He jotted something down and showed it to Trudy. "Are these the numbers you saw on the lady's arm?"

She stared at it for a few seconds, then nodded and put her thumb in her mouth.

"Are you sure?" Josh asked.

She nodded again. I grabbed the paper out of his hands and read it.

Josh: 857-555-4820

I met my brother-in-law's blue-eyed gaze. "What's this? Your telephone number?"

"Yeah."

"Why would your phone number be tattooed on my sister's arm?"

"It wasn't tattooed," he replied. "I just wrote it there, with a gel pen."

"When?" I couldn't understand this. Not at all.

"It's kind of a weird story," Josh replied hesitantly.

I turned to Holly and she grimaced. "I'm sorry, Riley. It is weird. That's why we never told anyone about it. Not ever."

"Told anyone *what*?" I asked.

She regarded her husband warily. "We have to tell them."

Josh nodded. "Margie, you might want to take Trudy to bed."

"You'll tell me later?" she whispered.

He and Holly agreed. Margie left the room and they suggested I sit down.

Forty

All I could do was pace around my kitchen while I strained to get a handle on this. "I've heard about these things before," I said, "but I never knew anyone who'd gone through it."

"Me neither," Josh replied. "Until it happened to me. There are still days when I think I dreamed the whole thing. I was pretty out of it when I woke up from the coma."

According to the story Josh had just related to me, after he was rushed into surgery following the shooting two years ago, his heart stopped beating on the operating table. He then floated upwards, out of his body, and was able to witness and recount things that happened during the surgery—things he never could have known from his vantage point on the table because he had been clinically dead.

"When I came to," Josh continued, "Leah was there in my room. She said she worked in the hospital as a resident doctor and I had no reason to doubt her. I hadn't seen her in years, not since we were kids. We talked about the past when we all used to live on the same street. She told me about what happened to you after your family moved to Boston and why you went to prison, and that's when I wrote my phone number on her arm—so we wouldn't lose touch again. When I was discharged, I went to your parents' house to see Leah, but I met Holly instead."

Holly squeezed Josh's shoulder. "I had to tell him that Leah had passed away. That's when we figured out that she had died on the same night he was brought in by ambulance after the shooting. We thought maybe she'd been having an out-of-body experience too, at the same time, and somehow they connected with each other in the hospital. That's the only thing that makes any sense."

"Makes sense?" I sat down again and stared at each of them in turn. "You're telling me Leah was a ghost and you talked to her."

Josh slowly nodded.

"That sounds crazy."

"We know."

"Why didn't you ever tell me this?" I asked Holly.

"Because, like you said…it sounds crazy."

"Yeah, but…I wish you'd told me anyway."

Learning that my older sister had died had been one of worst moments of my life because before that, I'd been estranged from my family for more than a decade. No one had even told me she was sick, nor had I been invited to her funeral.

But I couldn't let myself get mired in the past. Not now, when it appeared that my four-year-old daughter had somehow had an encounter with the ghost of my dead sister—an aunt she'd never met in this life.

More importantly, I had to stay focused on what mattered most: getting my newborn baby back from whomever took her.

It occurred to me suddenly that if Trudy had spoken to Leah, then the kidnapper had never come to my home. The so-called "lead" was no good. The person we were looking for was not a brown-haired woman with a ponytail and a tattoo on her arm. It was someone else entirely.

I cupped my forehead in a hand and lamented the fact that we had nothing now. *Nothing.* The trail was cold as ice and the cops were wasting their time, searching for irrelevant biblical references when the tattoo was nothing but my brother-in-law's phone number in Boston.

"What am I going to do?" I asked, bowing my head in defeat. "I can't call the cops and tell them it was a false alarm—that the reason they found no prints was because it was the ghost of my dead sister who came to my house that morning, not the kidnapper."

"You have to tell them," Josh said. "Otherwise they'll be running around the city on a wild goose chase when they need to be looking for other leads."

"They'll think I'm insane," I said. "They'll think I orchestrated all this."

"Why would they think that?" Holly asked.

I gave her a look. "I already have a prison record. This won't help matters any." My gut turned over sickeningly.

Holly started waving her hands around. "I think you're losing sight of the facts here."

"What *facts?*" I asked, feeling all the hope drain from my body.

"The fact that Leah was here in your house for some reason when your baby was kidnapped. If she came here to talk to Trudy, maybe there was a reason. Maybe she knows something."

I shook my head quickly. "First of all, I'm not ready to accept that a *ghost* came here to warn us..." I stopped talking suddenly as I remembered the dream I'd had in the hospital the morning of my daughter's disappearance—of being shaken awake by Leah after she'd knocked frantically on the window of the ICU.

"Or maybe I need to consider it. But why wouldn't Leah just tell *me*? Why tell a four-year-old who can't read or write or put two and two together."

"Because you can't *see* her," Holly replied, almost scolding me.

"I saw her in a dream yesterday morning in the hospital. I dreamed she was shaking me to wake me up."

"But she didn't say anything to you? And you haven't seen her or dreamed of her since?"

"No." I turned my eyes to Josh and stared at him intently. "But *you* can see her when you're awake, can't you? You saw her when you woke up from your coma."

He leaned an elbow on the table and rested his temple on his thumb. "Sorry. I wish I could. Believe me I've tried, many times over the past couple of years. That's why I've always wondered if I dreamed the whole thing, because I never saw her again. Not after those first few days in the hospital when I regained consciousness. Then it was only in dreams."

I stood up and gripped the back of my chair. "So what are we supposed to do? Call in a medium? Hold a séance? Or go buy a Ouija board?"

I was dumbfounded when Holly and Josh appeared to be considering those ideas.

"No." I began to pace. "This is absurd. Trudy must have remembered pictures of Leah that she saw in Boston last Christmas. I'm sure Mom talked about her. She probably dreamed it."

"That wouldn't explain how she could see Josh's phone number on Leah's arm," Holly said.

I bowed my head. "I'm sorry, Josh, but you can't write your phone number on the arm of a ghost, no matter how badly you want her to call you. It's just not possible. Like you said, you were pretty out of it when you woke up from your coma. You probably imagined it."

"Then how did he know all the things he knew about our family?" Holly argued. "It was Josh who came to the house knowing you were out of prison. He gave me your contact information."

"Did Leah give it to you?" I asked him. "Did she whisper my address in your ear?"

"No," Josh replied. "I did some investigating on my own after I left the hospital."

"Then maybe you heard things about me over the years that you forgot about, and it came out of your sub-conscious when you woke up. You only *thought* Leah told you." I shut my eyes and rested my hands on my hips. "What are we doing? My baby was kidnapped out of the hospital and we're having a discussion about my dead sister coming back from the grave to deliver clues to us. Do you know how nuts that sounds?"

I moved to pick up the phone and dialed Detective Miller's number. Holly and Josh watched me in silence while I waited for him to answer.

"Hi, Miller? It's Riley James. I have some bad news about the lead you've been working on—the woman who supposedly came to my house."

"What is it?" he asked.

I turned my gaze to meet Holly's. "It wasn't anyone. It turns out my daughter thought she was talking to my sister Leah, who passed away a couple of years ago. Trudy identified her in a number of photos."

"Wait, I don't understand," Miller replied. "Your daughter was talking to a ghost?"

"That's right. Well, no…I think she must have dreamed it."

"Are you sure your sister's dead?" he asked.

I frowned. "What do you mean?"

"I mean…How did she die? Is it possible there was some kind of error, or could she have faked her death?"

"So she could kidnap my baby?" I scoffed. "No, that's not possible." I turned to Holly. "He's asking if there's any chance Leah faked her own death."

Holly rolled her eyes, stood up and held out her hand. "Let me talk to him." I handed her the phone. "Hi, Detective Miller. I'm Holly, Riley's sister. Please let me assure you that Leah did pass away two years ago. She had ALS, which is a neurodegenerative disease and she was sick for quite some time before her death. I was at her side when she passed, so there can be no doubt." Holly handed the phone back to me. "He wants to talk to you again."

"Did your sister have a twin?" Miller asked me.

My mother walked into the kitchen just then. I turned to her and covered the mouthpiece as I spoke. "Mom, I have the detective on the phone. He wants to know if Leah had a twin."

She shook her head in confusion. "Of course she didn't."

"Sorry, I had to ask." I spoke into the phone again. "Did you hear that? No twin. You're grasping at straws here."

"I'm just trying to cover all the bases," he explained. He grew quiet. "Hold on a minute, Riley…*What's that?*" I waited while he spoke to someone else. Then he returned to our conversation. "Stay by the phone," he said firmly. "We might have another lead. I'll call back as soon as I can."

Click. The line went dead.

Forty-one

With a rush of alarm, I set the cordless phone into the charging base and stared at it in a fog. "He said to wait by the phone. Then he hung up on me."

"Do you think they found her?" Mom asked, striding forward with urgency.

"I don't know. He said they might have another lead."

None of us spoke. No doubt we were all in shock. Or praying. We just sat or stood, staring at the phone.

I jumped when Danny appeared in the doorway. "I'm going to bed," he said.

"Okay." It took all my willpower to behave normally when I wanted to run outside and tackle something. "Did you turn off the television?"

"Yes. Goodnight." He hugged all of us and disappeared into his room, closing the door behind him.

"Is Trudy asleep?" I asked my mother.

"Yes. I read her a story and she was out like a light before I got five pages into it."

We continued to wait in the kitchen while seconds ticked by like minutes.

"Should you call him back?" Holly asked. "This is torture."

I glanced at the clock. "It's only been five minutes."

The phone rang. I immediately picked it up.

"Hello? Yes, it's me." Turning to the others, I whispered, "It's Miller."

"I don't want you to get your hopes up," he said, "but I just received some information that might give us something to go on. I'm checking it out right now."

"What is it?" I asked. "Can you tell me?"

Through the phone, I heard the sound of Miller's car door lock beep just before he opened the door. "There was a report filed this evening about a missing person who was last seen at the hospital. She was there as a patient for blood work early this morning and was supposed to stay for an appointment at noon but never showed up for that. She hasn't been seen since and her sister is worried because she has a brain tumor and hasn't been herself lately. Get this…It was in the report that she had a miscarriage not long ago but she doesn't remember having it. Apparently, even though she was no longer pregnant, she was fixing up the nursery this week. She bought a crib and hung curtains. Holmes and I are heading over there now to talk to the sister. I'm sending a team to the hospital as well."

"You think this woman might have taken our baby?"

"We don't know that for sure yet," Miller replied.

"Can I meet you there?" I asked. "Can I talk to the sister, too?"

"No, just stay put. Let me do my job. I'll get back to you as soon as I know anything. I have to go."

"Thanks." I hung up the phone and turned to my family. "He has another lead and it sounds strong. A woman went missing from the hospital yesterday. He said she has a brain tumor and had a miscarriage recently, but she has no memory of it."

My mother covered her mouth with a hand. "Oh, God… What if she's not sane?"

I raked my fingers through my hair and felt a muscle clench at my jaw. "I have to call Lois and tell her."

As I picked up the phone to dial the hospital, Josh stood up and laid a hand on my shoulder. "This is good news, Riley," he said. "It's a solid lead."

"Better than a ghost," I replied. "But still, I won't relax until I'm holding my baby in my arms."

Jenn
Waiting for Jake

❝**W**hat's your baby's name?" an older lady asked while she waited for her husband to collect their suitcases off the baggage carousel.

I adjusted the strap of the diaper bag on my shoulder and turned slightly to show off the baby's face inside the BABYBJÖRN carrier.

"Her name is Alyssa," I replied with a smile.

The woman touched her soft head. "She's so adorable. She must only be a few days old. I'm going to be a grandmother soon," she added with a sparkle of joy in her eye. "My son and his wife are expecting."

"Their first?" I asked.

"Yes—so it'll be a first for all of us."

The woman's husband arrived with their suitcases. "Ready to go?" he asked, giving me a curious look.

"Yes," the woman replied. She turned back to me. "Unless you need help getting your bags? My husband would be happy to pick them up for you if you like."

I shook my head. "No need. I don't have any bags here except for this one." I gestured to my diaper bag. "I'm just waiting for my husband's plane to land. He's coming home from Afghanistan tonight."

"Oh, isn't that wonderful?" she said. "He'll be excited to see you no doubt. Please thank him for us—for his bravery and service."

"That's very kind. I'll tell him."

The woman took hold of her suitcase handle and followed her husband toward the main doors.

Looking down at Alyssa sleeping soundly in the carrier, I felt an immense surge of excitement in my heart. "Wait until Jake sees you," I whispered to her. "He's going to be so happy."

I turned and wandered off.

I wasn't sure how much time had passed since I last fed Alyssa—it seemed like I'd been wandering around the airport for hours, so when she began to fuss, I searched for a place to breastfeed.

Glancing around, I spotted an empty bench in a semi-private alcove and moved to claim it. Once there, I opened the diaper bag, withdrew a blanket to cover myself, unfastened the buckles on the carrier and gently lifted Alyssa out to hold her in my arms.

Motherhood was still new to me and I found myself wrestling with feelings of insecurity and self-consciousness. Breastfeeding in public wasn't something I'd given much thought to when I was expecting—because that process had been rather brief—but here I was, alone and needing to feed this baby. I glanced around uncomfortably, then assured myself that this was a private enough location.

Still, I felt a twinge of anxiety as I unbuttoned my blouse beneath the flannel blanket and cradled Alyssa's head in my hand, guiding her to my breast. *Would this even work?*

Alyssa latched on quickly enough, but within seconds, she let go and turned her face away. I persisted, but she stubbornly rejected me, time and time again.

"What's wrong, sweetheart?" I gently asked. "I thought you were hungry. You *must* be."

She put her fist in her mouth and I let out a frustrated breath, wincing at the burning sensation on my nipples which were chafed and red from all these failed attempts to feed her.

It wasn't easy to accept that this didn't come naturally to me because I'd never entertained any fears that I wouldn't be good at breastfeeding. What can I say? I was a born optimist.

"Don't worry," I said, working hard to stay positive as I buttoned my blouse. "We'll get this, you and I, because we're not quitters. It just takes practice, that's all. I'll call the doctor as soon as we get home and ask about it. I must be doing something wrong."

She continued to fuss, however, and I didn't know what to do, how to make her happy. I picked her up and held her, conscious of people walking by with wheeled suitcases, glancing over at me with sympathy in their eyes.

I wished Jake were here. *Hurry and get home. I need you. I think I may have bitten off more than I can chew.*

It wasn't easy for me to admit that to myself.

Forty-three

"I don't know what to do," I whispered, growing more and more desperate as I sat on that bench in the airport, holding that screaming baby in my arms.

By then it was dark outside and I didn't know where my husband was or how I got there. My head was throbbing, but I didn't want to take any medication because I thought I was supposed to be breastfeeding and I wasn't sure how that might affect the baby. New mothers had to be so careful.

Glancing at the open diaper bag, I spotted a package of wipes and a few diapers and wondered if she needed to be changed. If that might help.

I stuffed the BABYBJÖRN carrier into the bag and took Alyssa in my arms to a family washroom with a sign that indicated there was a change table inside. I entered and locked the door behind me. It was a large, private washroom with a polyethylene change station attached to the wall and lowered on its hinges. I laid Alyssa upon it and kept my hand on her belly while I pulled a fresh diaper and wipes out of the bag.

Sure enough, when I finally removed her diaper, I saw that it was soiled. "There! I'm not a total failure at this after all," I said in a playful voice, kissing her cheek. "Maybe this was the problem the whole time."

As I cleaned her little bum and outfitted her in a fresh diaper, something strange began to happen. There was a buzzing sound in my head. A thick fog seemed to surround my thoughts.

Quickly I finished dressing the baby in her pink cotton sleeper, somehow knowing that I had to get her off this table—but it wasn't easy to maneuver her little feet into the leg holes. I was all thumbs. Even my tongue felt thick and unwieldy.

It was only in that moment that I noticed she wore a hospital identification band around her ankle. I stared at it, bewildered.

What was happening? Confusion swirled around me. I found myself wondering where I was and *who* I was. What was my name?

Then my muscles began to stiffen. I felt all twitchy inside and my heart fluttered like pigeon wings. Frightened and anxious, I wanted to call out for help but couldn't seem to find words that made any sense in the thick ball of wool inside my brain. I couldn't even get my vocal chords to work. Was there anyone out there? *Help! We need help!*

Knowing something terrible was happening to me, I looked down at the baby and had a frightening vision of her falling off the change table. *We have to get to the floor.*

But whose baby was it? Was it mine? No, it couldn't be. Where was I?

Carefully, with growing distress, I gathered the child into my bungling arms, shaking with feverish terror at the possibility that I might drop her, and somehow I managed to sink to my knees and set her gently on the floor beside me.

There...There, now...

Unable to control my movements, I stretched out in an involuntary fashion and squirmed awkwardly, helplessly, until my eyes rolled back in my head. Then my body began to convulse faster and I became imprisoned in a shuddering, tortuous, inescapable and merciless shell.

Sylvie

When the doorbell rang, I practically leaped out of my chair. I'd been waiting impatiently for the detective to arrive—the one who had called to follow up on Officer Jenkins's missing person's report.

In fact, I was surprised when he called because Jenkins hadn't seemed overly concerned by the situation. Earlier, I doubted he would even file the report, but he must have filed something because there were now two plainclothes detectives at my door—one male and one female.

I opened it quickly. "Hi. Are you Detective Miller?"

I glanced down at his badge which was clipped to his belt, then up at his face which I studied carefully in the hazy glare of the porch light. He was of medium height with strong features and dark eyes.

"Yes. You must be Sylvie?" He shook my hand. "This is my partner, Detective Holmes." Holmes was female, about six inches shorter than Miller, slim and petite. "Thanks for seeing us," he added. "Mind if we come in?"

"Please do." I stepped aside and opened the door wider. "I'm really glad you're here, actually. My sister's not home yet and it's not like her to ignore my texts or calls. Something's definitely wrong. I'm really worried. Did Officer Jenkins tell you she has a brain tumor?"

Miller wasn't looking at me, however. His eyes were perusing the house. He was looking all around at the floors, the walls and even the ceilings. Then he inclined his head to peer into the living room.

"She's not here," I said, feeling taken aback by his interest in the house as opposed to what I had to say. "She's missing, remember?"

"Just looking for clues," Miller explained, meeting my eyes at last with a warm and reassuring smile that unnerved me for some reason. Even the female detective seemed to be watching me intently, sizing me up.

"You guys seem a lot keener than the cop who came to my door earlier," I mentioned. "What's going on?"

Miller reached into his pocket for his notepad and pen. "The report said your sister had a miscarriage a few weeks ago, but she doesn't remember anything?"

"That's right."

"I'm sorry to hear that. It also said she continued to set up a nursery in the house, even after losing the baby. Is that correct as well?"

"Yes, just in the last few days."

He nodded and looked down at the notepad. "And when was the last time you saw her?"

"Last night, when we went to bed. We talked about her appointment for blood work this morning. She planned to take a cab. We texted each other throughout the day and she said she was fine. I assumed everything was okay, but I came home to a message on my answering machine that said she didn't show up for her checkup at noon. I don't know where she went after her blood work. I called the clinic and asked them if she mentioned anything about going anywhere, but they had no information. And I went to the hospital myself to look for her tonight, after Jenkins left. I walked through the whole place but she wasn't there."

Miller wrote a few things down and said, "Mind if I take a look at that nursery?"

"Sure," I replied, leading the way, "but I wouldn't exactly call it a nursery. It's mostly a storage room for a lot of junk since I moved in here."

Both detectives followed me down the hall. I opened the door and they walked in. The female detective examined the labels on the new curtains and baby blanket in the crib.

"The report said your sister is married and her husband is coming home from Afghanistan tonight?" Miller asked.

"Yes, I think so, but I haven't heard from him yet. I sent him a text but he must still be in the air."

"So neither your sister, nor her husband, are responding to your calls?"

A shiver of unease snaked up my spine as I recognized a note of suspicion in his tone. I also saw mistrust in the way the female detective was looking at me.

Suddenly I didn't feel like the victim. I felt like the guilty party.

"What's happening here?" I asked as they continued to survey the contents of the room.

Miller's cell phone rang just then. He withdrew it from his jacket pocket. "Miller here." He listened and exchanged a look with Detective Holmes. "Good work. Send someone over there now to check the security tapes. Yes, we're still here talking to her sister. Let me know if you find anything else."

He hung up the phone, stared at me for a moment, and addressed me directly. "I'm afraid we have a bit of a situation here, Sylvie."

"What is it?" I asked as a wave of panic rippled up my spine.

"Your sister's not the only person who went missing today," he replied. "We've been working on another case as well—a newborn baby that was taken from the same hospital your sister went to for blood work. The baby was taken from the nursery sometime between 6:00 and 9:00 a.m. Do you know anything about that?"

Bewildered, I shook my head. "What are you suggesting? That my sister kidnapped that baby?" When he gave no reply, I said, "So you're not here because she's missing. You're here because she's the suspect in a child abduction case?"

Again, Miller simply stared at me. I sensed he was waiting for me to answer my own question or start spilling out a waterfall of information.

"Who was on the phone just now?" I asked.

Thankfully he was upfront with me. "One of the detectives on the case called to tell me that your sister used her credit card at Walmart this afternoon, here in the city. She purchased a diaper bag, a baby blanket, and one of those infant carriers, as well as a few other items."

I stared at him in disbelief. "Well, at least she's not lying in a ditch somewhere. Not that *you'd* care."

"We do care," Detective Holmes said, striding forward to stand beside Miller. "If your sister is suffering from mental illness, we want to help her and make sure that she's safe."

"It's not mental illness," I replied. "It's a brain tumor, and I give you my word that she would never do anything like this under normal circumstances. Seriously, you have to believe me. Just to give you some perspective, she suffered a miscarriage and didn't remember having it."

I wondered suddenly if I should be saying things like that. Maybe I should be calling a lawyer.

The two detectives shared a look. "Can you tell us where you think she might have gone?" Miller asked.

Realizing there was a missing child in the picture—and my sister really needed to be found—I labored to remember everything we'd talked about the night before.

"I don't know. She had every intention of going to her doctor's appointment at noon. If she got confused and took a baby, thinking it was hers, I would have expected her to come home with it and put it in the crib she just bought. It doesn't make sense that she'd go anywhere else because I'm certain this wouldn't have been premeditated. She would never plot to abduct someone else's child and make off with it. She's not a criminal. She's the nicest person you'd ever want to know. Besides, she can't remember things. She forgets." I felt heat rush to my cheeks. "Oh God, what if she has a seizure?"

Miller frowned. "She has seizures? How often?"

"She's only ever had two," I replied. "It happened less than a week ago but the doctor gave her medication to prevent them from happening again until she could have the surgery."

"Surgery to remove the tumor?" Holmes asked.

"Yes. It's scheduled for the day after tomorrow."

"Has she been taking the medication?" Miller asked.

"I think so. I've watched her a few times. Let me check." I ran to the kitchen where she kept her pills and opened the bottle to look inside. "Most of them are gone," I said. "She takes them right here at the sink."

To my surprise, Holmes pointed at the green houseplant on the windowsill. "I don't suppose she thought they'd make good fertilizer?"

Lifting my eyes, I nearly swallowed my gum at the sight of a small pile of pills on top of the dirt. "What the heck?" I picked one up to examine it. "This is crazy. I watched her open the bottle, put the pill on her tongue and drink the water."

"Any chance she might have put the pill on her tongue," Holmes asked, "didn't like the taste of it, and gave it to the plant instead?"

I sighed with defeat. "Maybe. Oh Lord." Feeling a surge of panic, I turned to Miller. "This is really bad. She's sick. She could be passed out somewhere. And if she took a baby…Pray God, she didn't…" I covered my face with my hands. "Why didn't she just come home? Or at least call?"

Miller handed me his card. "Get in touch with me right away if you hear from her. Even if she didn't take the baby, someone else did, so we need to know everything."

They made a move to leave so I led them to the front door. When I opened it, however, my jaw fell open at the sight of Jake, in full fatigues, walking up the steps. A cab was just pulling away from the curb.

There was no sight of Jenn.

"You're home," I said, pausing in the doorway. "Thank God." I strode forward and wrapped my arms around his neck.

Army bag in hand, Jake hugged me while glancing over my shoulder at the two detectives. "Where's Jenn?" he asked. "And who are these people?"

I pulled Jake into the house where the detectives were waiting. "This is Detective Miller and Detective Holmes. They're here because Jenn went missing today."

Jake's eyebrows pulled together. "Missing...What do you mean?"

I proceeded to explain the situation while the detectives watched and waited for Jake's response.

"Christ!" he said. "How could this happen?"

"When was the last time you spoke to your wife?" Miller asked, reaching for his pen and flipping open his notepad.

Jake set down his bag. "We talked on the phone just before I boarded my flight in Dubai. That was last night, I guess. She said she had an appointment to get blood work done today."

"Have you heard from her since then?" Miller asked him.

"I got a couple of texts from her—maybe about ten hours ago—but I've been in the air so my phone was on flight mode. I texted her back when I was waiting for my connection in Atlanta, but she didn't respond. I figured her phone was dead or she was sleeping. I was disappointed when she didn't meet me at the air-port just now, but I figured it was because my flight was delayed. My schedule got messed up."

"Why didn't you call the house when you landed?" I asked Jake. "I could have picked you up."

"I did call," he explained. "No one answered. I didn't bother to leave a message."

I glanced back at the phone. "I must have been at the hospital when you called. I was looking for her."

"But you didn't find her?" Jake said, beginning to pace. "What the hell, Sylvie? No one knows where she is? She has a brain tumor!" He turned to me. "How could you let her go to the hospital alone? Why weren't you with her?"

"I had an exam," I explained. "We talked it over last night and she convinced me she'd be fine. She's been really good all week and I thought she was taking her medication. I'm so sorry, Jake."

With mounting anger, he continued to pace around the kitchen. "God...How long has she been gone?"

Detective Miller slipped his notepad into his pocket. "We have a record of her using her credit card at Walmart this afternoon around 1:30 p.m. So she was still in the city at that time. We have a team over there now, looking at the security camera recordings and asking questions."

Jake regarded Miller with concern. "We have to find her. She's sick and she's pregnant, too."

Miller and Holmes both glanced at me curiously.

"Oh, Jake..." I moved to lay my hand on his arm. "I'm so sorry about this. You better come in here and sit down. I have to tell you something."

"What is it?" he asked as I led him into the living room.

"It's about the baby."

I wasn't surprised when Miller and Holmes followed us. No doubt they wanted to hear this, too.

Riley

After relaying the latest developments to Lois in the hospital, I hung up the phone and moved into the living room to sit alone for a few minutes. Holly rose from the table, followed me and sat down on the sofa.

"How did she take the news?" Holly asked.

All I could do was shrug, because I'd never known my wife to be so guarded and silent. She was always an open book. Today, however, was a different story.

"She'll come around," Holly said. "And you can't blame yourself, Riley. You were up for days, taking care of your wife during her labor, which was no easy thing. When it was over, you had to sleep. You couldn't have known this would happen. Besides, it's the hospital's fault, not yours."

I managed to nod my head. "I just hope Lois sees it that way, eventually."

"She will. Be patient. She's scared right now."

"I'm scared, too," I replied, slouching down on the sofa to rest my head on the back cushions and stare up at the ceiling. "What if they don't find this woman? Or what if they do, and she's done something terrible? I'm not sure if Lois would ever be able to get over that, much less forgive *me,* if something happens to our baby."

"She'll have to," Holly replied, "because it was no more your fault than it was hers. You'd both been through hell during her delivery. But that doesn't matter because they're going to find your baby. Everything's going to be okay."

A movement at the corner of my eye caused me to lift my head. There stood Trudy on the carpet with her thumb in her mouth, her oversized rag doll hugged close to her little body.

"Hey kiddo." I rose to my feet and picked her up. She wrapped her legs around my waist. "What's the matter? Couldn't sleep?"

Trudy shook her head and pulled her thumb out of her mouth. She spoke weepily. "The lady woke me up."

I felt a sudden eruption of goose bumps over my skin. "What lady? The one with the numbers on her arm?"

Trudy nodded. "She shook me hard, Daddy. I didn't like it. It scared me." Her bottom lip quivered and her eyes filled with tears.

I turned to Holly who quickly stood. She approached us and rubbed Trudy's back in a comforting way. "Did she say anything to you?"

Trudy rested her cheek on my shoulder. "She made me get out of bed."

"Why?" I asked.

"To tell you she's at the airport."

"*Who's* at the airport?" I asked insistently, shifting Trudy in my arms to prevent her from falling back to sleep.

"Try to remember, sweetheart." Holly rubbed Trudy's back. "It's very important. Did she tell you who?"

Trudy stuck her thumb back in her mouth. "My sister."

Immediately, I carried Trudy to the kitchen and passed her to my mother, who was still seated at the table. I squatted down to ask my daughter one more question. "Did she tell you *where* at the airport? Think hard, Trudy. Please."

Trudy shook her head and I knew she had no more information to give. "Take care of the kids," I said to my mom. "I have to go."

"Why?" she asked, her face turning ashen.

"To get my child. God help us, what if she's getting on a plane?"

"What if *who's* getting on a plane?" my mother asked with distress as I grabbed my keys off a hook on the wall and ran to the door.

I was vaguely aware of Josh and Holly hurrying to follow me out.

CHAPTER

Forty-six

❧

Inserting my key into the ignition, I waited a brief second or two for Josh and Holly to get into my car and slam their doors, then I sped out of the driveway.

I passed my phone to Josh who sat in the front beside me. "Call Detective Miller and tell him we're on our way to the airport. Tell him the kidnapper's there."

While I drove at a fast clip out of our neighborhood, Josh found the number in my recent contacts and dialed it. "Hello? Detective Miller? This is Josh Wallace. I'm Riley James's brother-in-law. We just received a tip that the kidnapper is at the airport with the baby. We're on our way there now...Yes, that's right... No, we don't have any more information than that. Thanks. We'll see you there."

Josh ended the call. As he reached for his seatbelt, he glanced over his shoulder at Holly, who sat next to the empty baby seat in the back. "Are you buckled in?"

"Yes," she replied.

I checked my rearview mirror, then hit the gas, keeping my eyes peeled for oncoming traffic—or cops—as I approached an intersection and drove straight through a red light.

For once, luck was with me. I didn't get pulled over. Cops were never overly forgiving when they checked your license and discovered you were an ex-con.

My tires skidded to a screeching halt at the passenger drop-off zone in front of the airport terminal. The three of us spilled out of the car and pushed through the revolving doors to the departure area...where we stopped dead in our tracks and looked around.

So many people...

"Let's split up." I reached for my phone. "I'm calling Miller now in case the woman went through security. Look everywhere. Stop anyone with a baby."

Moving at a brisk pace while scanning left and right for women with infants, I spoke into the phone. "Pick up, Miller. Pick up."

At last he answered my call. "Miller here."

"It's Riley," I said. "I'm at the airport but I'm worried she's getting on a plane and might have already gone through security. I can't get past security to check without buying a ticket, which will take some time. Are you on your way?"

"We're just pulling in," he said. "We'll take care of this, Riley, and she may not be getting on a plane. I suspect she's there to meet an arrival."

"What do you mean?" I asked. "How do you know that?"

"Because I just met her husband. He's in the military service and came home from Afghanistan tonight for her surgery. He got off a flight from Atlanta an hour ago. And get this...she never told him about her miscarriage."

"Thanks." I ended the call and ran toward the baggage carousels.

Maybe I was running too fast. Maybe I was distracted. Or maybe my shoelace was untied. I have no explanation for what happened and why it happened when it did. All I know is that I stumbled and fell, as if someone had tripped me. My chin hit the floor, my teeth clacked together and a searing pain reverberated from my jaw to the very top of my skull.

Rolling to my side, I struggled to get my bearings in a world that was spinning around and around. Suddenly I found myself staring up at three faces—all strangers—crowded around me.

"Geez, are you okay?" some guy with dreadlocks asked.

Feeling dazed, I rolled to my stomach, rose up on all fours in a clumsy attempt to get to my feet. There was a metallic taste of blood in my mouth. I spit onto the floor.

"I don't think you should get up," the guy said, concerned.

"I'm all right." I rose to my feet and staggered sideways.

"You're bleeding," a young girl said, pointing at my lip.

I touched it with a finger.

"Go get him some tissues," her mother suggested. "There's a washroom right there."

Feeling slightly dizzy, I watched the girl grasp the door lever and jiggle it. She turned around with a blank expression. "It's locked."

"There must be someone in there," her mother replied as she dug into her purse. "I might have some Kleenex…"

Then, like some kind of beacon in the night, I heard a baby squeak. All my senses came alive and the dizziness vanished. The whole world went quiet and still. I felt as if I could hear a pin drop on the other side of the airport.

I stood motionless and listened.

There.

Again…

A small pithy cry, barely audible in the noise of the terminal.

I ran to the bathroom door and rattled the lever handle. When I couldn't open it, I began to knock urgently. "Hello? Is anyone in there? Can you open up please? It's an emergency."

No response. I waited a few seconds and heard another squeak. I pressed my ear to the door. "Is there a baby in there?"

Still no answer. My breathing accelerated and I felt an uncontrollable trembling in all my bones and muscles.

"*Open the door!*" I shouted as I began to pound violently with the edge of my fist, squeezed tight as a vise.

Scarcely conscious of the young girl backing away from me in wide-eyed fear, I rammed my shoulder up against the door, again and again, fighting to force it open. Then I heard it more clearly. The sound of a baby, now crying with all the power in her tiny little lungs.

I recognized that cry. It was my daughter's. It was the same cry I'd heard when she came back from the brink of death in the OR.

Taking a step back, I attempted to kick the door open with my boot. *Bang, bang, bang!*

"Buddy relax," the guy with dreadlocks said, approaching me from behind. "There's someone in there. I'm sure they'll be out soon."

"Get security!" I shouted at everyone, full of rage. "I need this door open! *Now!*"

With terror-filled eyes, the guy took off to find someone to help.

I continued to ram the side of my body up against the door until I was grabbed by the arms, pulled away and forced to the floor with my hands behind my back. I felt the familiar, soul-crushing sensation of handcuffs clicking around my wrists. "*No!*" I shouted.

Lying on my stomach, with my cheek on the cold hard tiles, I watched the scene unfold around me as if it were happening in slow motion.

Cops were everywhere. Running. Shouting. Telling people to move back. Someone unlocked the door with a key. It swung open. I saw a woman's legs on the floor. They weren't moving.

"It's Jenn Nichols," someone said as two cops rushed into the room and knelt down to attend to her.

I heard my baby crying.

My stomach muscles clenched tight and I gritted my teeth in desperation, fighting to move but there were two firm knees pressing into my spine.

Then Holmes, the female detective, emerged from behind the bathroom door holding my baby in her arms.

Someone freed my hands from the cuffs and set me loose. It was Miller. I scrambled to my feet and for the first time, reached out to hold my child.

Looking down at my daughter's face, I was overcome with relief and a joy so profound, the whole world turned into a kaleidoscope of color before my eyes. I sank to my knees and laughed and cried as I bent my head to kiss her soft, warm head.

Thank you, God. Thank you for saving the life of my child and for bringing her home to us.

As soon as I was able to collect myself, I looked up and saw Holly running down the escalators, pushing past curious bystanders. She reached the ground floor and sprinted toward me, but a police officer held out his arm to stop her.

"It's okay," I explained. "She's my sister."

He let her pass and she dropped to her knees in front of me. "I can't believe it. You found her." She leaned close to look at her. "Is she all right?"

"I think so," I replied. "Holmes said she was on the floor in the bathroom, wrapped in a blanket."

"And you're sure it's your baby?"

"We're sure. She's still wearing the identity bracelet from the hospital and the numbers match the one I'm wearing." I showed her the band on my wrist.

Besides that, there was no doubt in my mind that this was my daughter. I felt some sort of extraordinary paternal instinct.

"Your lip…" Holly said, pointing at it. "You're going to need stitches." She looked around. "I wonder if someone has a first aid kit."

I awkwardly reached into my pocket for my phone. "I need to call Lois."

Letting go of the notion of treating my lip, Holly held out her arms. "I can hold her for you."

I shook my head. "No, I don't want to let go of her just yet." Still on my knees, sitting on my heels, I used my sleeve to wipe the blood from my chin and managed to dial Lois's number.

"Hello?" she answered.

"Hey babe, we found her," I said without any preliminaries. "She's all right. I have her here in my arms. She's fine."

"Oh, my God!" Lois immediately burst into tears. "*You found her?* You really have her?"

"Yes, and she's beautiful. I can't wait for you to see her."

"She's okay?"

"She's probably hungry, but she seems fine, yes. I'm bringing her back to the hospital to make sure."

Lois said nothing for a moment though I could hear her weeping, so I waited.

"Where was she?" Lois asked when she stopped crying. "Where did you find her?"

"We're at the airport," I replied. "And Miller was right. It was the woman with the brain tumor who had her."

"The one who went missing from the hospital this morning?" Lois asked. "Did they arrest her?"

A team of paramedics came running by with a stretcher. They hurried to where Jenn Nichols was lying, immobile, on the floor inside the washroom.

"Not yet," I replied. "She's not conscious." My gut churned with dread. "I'm not even sure if she's alive. The paramedics just came."

"Why is she unconscious? Was there a standoff or something?"

"No. We have no idea what happened. All we know is that she was locked in a private bathroom when I found them. I'm guessing she might have collapsed in there. She's supposed to have brain surgery the day after tomorrow."

"You're kidding me," Lois replied with genuine concern. "But why would she kidnap a baby when she's about to have brain surgery?"

I looked down at my daughter and felt another rush of joy. How immensely blessed I was, to be holding her in my arms.

"I don't know what the woman's story is, but Miller suspects she came to the airport to meet her husband who was coming home from Afghanistan tonight. He's a soldier."

I watched the paramedics lift Jenn Nichols onto the stretcher. Lois grew quiet. "Wait a minute...You said *you* found them?"

"Yes. I sort of got a tip about where they were."

"From whom?" Lois asked.

Finding my balance, I rose to my feet. "It's a long story. I promise I'll tell you everything, but first I want to bring our baby to you."

The paramedics pushed the stretcher toward the ambulance which was parked outside. "Is she alive?" I asked as they passed by.

"Yes," one of them told me but she offered no more than that.

I followed for a few frantic strides to get a look at the woman's face beneath the oxygen mask—the woman who had taken my child mere hours after she was born.

Maybe it was not my finest hour, but I felt no sympathy. My heart began to race with rancor. Part of me wanted to rip the mask off her face and throw it aside, shake this woman senseless. *How could you?*

Josh arrived and laid his hand on my shoulder, pulling me from the violence of my imaginings.

"Thank God, she's okay," Josh said. "You did good."

I don't know what happened in the seconds after that. My mind was still spinning.

In due course, we spoke to Miller about returning to the hospital with the baby. Holmes inspected the blood on my face and insisted that she carry my child to Miller's unmarked police vehicle, in case I passed out or something. I gave my keys to Josh, and Holmes sent an officer with him and Holly to fetch the safety seat in the back of my car.

Holmes and Miller then escorted all of us to the hospital.

Along the way, as I sat in the back seat of Miller's car with my baby girl, I felt distracted the entire time—and full of vengeful rage whenever I looked out the window.

Fifty

Miller called the hospital on our behalf to let them know our baby had been found. I was instructed to take her straight to pediatrics to be checked over and to confirm her identity. Other than being hungry, she was perfectly fine—and she *was* ours.

As soon as I walked through the door of Lois's room, she sat up in bed and covered her face with her hands. Carol was there as well. She stood from her chair.

"I'm so happy!" Lois cried, holding out her arms.

I gave our baby to my wife and stood by her side as she wept tears of joy. Vaguely I was aware of my mother-in-law leaving us alone in the room.

"I was so afraid I'd never even know what she looked like," Lois cried. "Never hold her in my arms. Never hear the sound of her little voice…" Her watery eyes lifted to meet mine and she pointed at me. "What happened to your lip?"

"I was in a hurry to find her," I replied. "I fell at the airport, but it's fine. I'll get it looked at."

She regarded me with tenderness and concern, and her eyes filled with tears again. "You're my hero," she said. "I was such a mess today."

Overcome with love for my wife and newborn daughter—and feeling a deep sense of relief that she was safely returned to us—I reached for Lois's hand and pressed it to my cheek.

"I was a mess, too," I said as I drew back, recalling my dangerous moment of weakness in the bar with that shot of Jack Daniels.

Lois turned her attention to our child who was rooting toward her breast. "She's hungry." I helped Lois untie the back of her hospital gown. Gently, she pulled our baby close to her heart. "That's it," Lois whispered, maneuvering our baby around to find a comfortable position. It took a moment or two, but soon she was drinking her fill.

Lois looked up at me and smiled. "Proud-mama moment here. She's doing it like a pro."

I smiled in return and pulled up a chair to sit beside her.

"Wow," Lois said, "she's *really* hungry."

As I sat in the quiet hospital room watching my wife and daughter become acquainted with each other in the most intimate way, I had to choke back the urge to cry. I was completely overwhelmed by the miracle of life and astounded by how lucky we were to have our child back with us—when it could have so easily gone another way.

I couldn't bear to think about all the "what ifs."

"Riley," Lois said, gazing across at me intently. "We haven't given her a name yet. I can't believe we went so long without deciding."

I gently closed my hand around her wrist. "Maybe sometimes the right name just needs a little time to reveal itself."

She narrowed her eyes with curiosity. "What do you have in mind?"

Sitting back and tapping a finger on the arm of the chair, I tentatively asked, "What do you think of the name...*Leah*?"

"After your sister?" she replied, sounding surprised.

"Do you like it?"

"I *love* it. I can't believe we didn't think of it before."

I was pleased she didn't hesitate. Not for a single second. "But what did you mean about the name 'revealing itself'?"

I sighed with exhaustion and began to wonder if certain events of the past twelve hours had been figments of my imagination, or a lucid dream of some kind.

But no...Holly was there. She'd also heard what Trudy said.

"When I was at the airport," I explained, sitting forward in my chair, "and you and I were talking on the phone, you asked how I knew where to look for Jenn Nichols." Lois inclined her head, waiting patiently for me to continue. "It's kind of an interesting story, and I don't know if you're going to believe it."

"Try me," she said as our daughter fell happily to sleep in her arms.

"All right then." I leaned back again and relaxed in a lazy sprawl. "It all started with Trudy's description of the woman who came to our house. Remember she said she had a tattoo on her arm?" Lois nodded. "It took us a while to figure that one out, and we never would have known what it meant if Josh and Holly hadn't arrived when they did..."

❦

After explaining the extent of Trudy's so-called encounters with her dearly departed Auntie Leah, I ventured to the ER to get a few stitches in my lower lip, then spent the night in Lois's room with our beautiful baby. Wrapped tightly in each other's arms on her bed, we slept with little Leah in a bassinet beside us. After what we'd both been through, no one at the hospital dared to argue with that arrangement, and the pediatrician was more than willing to make a "house call" to examine Leah in our room.

The following morning, Miller came by to talk to me. He asked if we could speak privately.

I said, "Sure," and followed him into the corridor.

He led me toward the visitors' lounge. "I thought you should know that Jenn Nichols is in custody, here in the hospital. She was admitted last night to recover from a seizure."

"So that's what happened in the airport bathroom?" I confirmed as I walked with him down the hall. "Will she be okay?"

It was the polite, socially responsible question to ask, but deep down, a part of me was not sorry she was suffering. To me—as a father who had just recovered his newborn daughter from a kidnapper—it felt like some sort of perfectly rendered poetic justice.

"We're not sure about that yet," Miller replied. "She was unconscious for most of the night and just woke up an hour ago. We tried questioning her but she's pretty groggy. She barely makes sense when she tries to talk. Her husband, sister and mother are with her now."

As I contemplated the idea of her family at her side, I tried to swallow an innate urge to become empathetic, because I didn't *want* to feel sorry for her. This woman had abducted my child. What if I hadn't known to look for them at the airport? Where would we be right now? Would my child even be alive?

I endeavored to redirect my thoughts, however, because I was doing it again—obsessing over all the possible "what ifs."

"Did she tell you anything about why she did it?" I asked.

Miller stopped when we reached the private lounge area. He gestured with a hand for me to enter. As soon as we were seated, he crossed one leg over the other. "That's what's going to make this case complicated," he told me. "Unfortunately, Ms. Nichols has no memory of anything that happened yesterday and she's still not able to explain much more than that. The doctors say she's suffering from post-seizure fatigue but that she will eventually come around and become more coherent."

"So what are you telling me?" I asked. "That you can't charge her because she can't remember what she did?"

"I'm not saying that at all," Miller replied. "The evidence against her is overwhelming. We know beyond any doubt that she took your child from the hospital yesterday. We have security video recordings of her at Walmart with the baby in her arms, purchasing a car seat and diaper bag and other items, and we also have a report from a hospital patient who saw her yesterday morning after leaving the blood drawing clinic, and then saw her again later with the baby in her arms, walking out. So there's no question she abducted your child, Riley. Rest assured, we will be pursuing this aggressively."

I inhaled deeply with relief and let it out. "But will she be convicted if she can't remember anything and has a brain tumor? Forgive me, Miller, I'm not an expert on the law or on neurology, but wouldn't a jury be sympathetic to that? And what about pleading insanity? Do you know anything about the symptoms or effects of the tumor? Could it cause someone to do something like that? Or did she consciously plan it? You said she didn't tell her husband about the miscarriage. Isn't it possible she might have wanted a replacement baby?"

"Anything's possible," Miller replied, nodding his head, "and we're gathering evidence, talking to a lot of people, including her neurologist. Thankfully her family is cooperating. They want us to know everything about the tumor."

"What does the neurologist say?" I asked.

Miller uncrossed his legs and sat forward. "He explained that the tumor is pressing on both the frontal and temporal lobes. He said the pressure on the frontal lobe causes confusion and irrational behavior, loss of normal inhibitions, and complete memory loss. Confusion at this level—leading her to mistake another baby for her own—is extreme and not at all common in most brain tumor patients, but it is possible. It's also possible that she knew it wasn't her child, but didn't think it was wrong to take her. The doctor said patients can lose all sense of what's appropriate. For instance, they can urinate in public and see no reason why not to."

I considered this for a moment. "You said she was scheduled to have surgery tomorrow to remove the tumor?"

"That's right."

"Will they go ahead with that?"

"Yes. The doctors are insisting."

I rubbed the back of my neck and thought about what that would mean. "Will she remember what she did *after* she has the surgery?"

Miller looked down at his shoes. "Not likely."

Feeling weary and disheartened, I rose from my seat and walked to the window to look outside. "I feel bad for what's happening to this woman," I said. "Honestly, I do, but there has to be consequences. A person can't just get away with stealing someone else's baby out of a hospital. Someone has to be held accountable for that. The hospital at the very least. Why in the world would her doctors let her out of their sight if she was this far gone?"

"I agree," Miller replied. "Have you spoken to a lawyer yet?"

"Not yet," I replied, lowering my gaze. "I've been kind of preoccupied."

"Of course." Miller stood up. "Listen, you should definitely talk to someone about what happened. In the meantime, we'll continue to gather evidence and wait and see what happens with the surgery."

My eyes lifted. "What do you mean, wait and see?"

He slowly approached and laid a hand on my shoulder. "It's a high risk operation, Riley. The family has a lot of praying to do." With that, he squeezed my shoulder and left the room.

few hours later, I left Lois and the baby alone with Carol and ventured to the cafeteria to grab a bowl of soup and a salad. Choosing a table by the window, I set down my tray, paused a moment to calm my mind and picked up my spoon.

The time alone provided me with a much-needed opportunity to think more deeply about everything that had occurred over the past twenty-four hours. I thought about how close I had come to losing my child and facing a lifetime of insurmountable grief.

In the wake of all that, I'd almost resorted to taking an alcoholic drink—something I hadn't done in over a decade—but if there ever was a situation that would put me in danger of succumbing to that temptation, this had been it.

The stress and fear of losing my child had eclipsed anything I'd ever experienced or could imagine, so the fact I'd possessed the strength to make it through that, meant I could make it through anything. That, at least, was a comforting thought.

On the other side of the coin, the woman who had kidnapped my baby had a brain tumor and was facing life-threatening surgery in the morning, and part of me—*most of me*—felt no sympathy. I wanted to be sympathetic, but I was still so angry. Rationally I knew it was a horrible, tragic thing she was going through, and for anyone else I would feel badly for the family, but I couldn't seem to shake my protective emotions as a father.

When someone hurts your child, is it ever possible to forgive?

My musings were interrupted by the tentative approach of a man and a woman. They stopped at my table and simply stood there. My gut twisted into a knot because I knew who these people were.

The woman cleared her throat. "Excuse me," she said. "Are you Riley James?"

"Yes." I sat back in my chair, wiped my mouth with a napkin, folded it and laid it on the tray.

She gestured toward her companion. "I'm Sylvie and this is my brother-in-law, Jake. Jenn Nichols is my sister." She looked at me directly, her eyes two piercing rays of hopeful expectation.

This caused my heart to beat like a mallet because last night I'd imagined myself violently shaking their loved one out of her stupor until she explained herself to me. What did they even want from me? Did they hope to deliver a stirring sob story that would wear me down and make me feel sorry enough not to charge their sister with kidnapping? It wasn't even up to me. What Jenn Nichols did was a criminal offense, which meant they'd have to plead their case to the judge and jury.

The sister—*Sylvie, was it?*—cleared her throat again and spoke cautiously. "Could we sit down for a minute?"

Shrugging a shoulder, I replied coolly, "Be my guest."

Almost immediately, I wished I'd said no or gotten up and walked away because this was a complicated situation and I didn't want to screw up Miller's investigation. But there had to be a reason I *didn't* walk away. Maybe I was curious. Or maybe I just wanted to watch them squirm.

"I can only imagine what you must have gone through yesterday," Sylvie said with a look of genuine compassion in her eyes. When I gave no reply, she shifted uneasily in her chair. "This is difficult. I'm not even sure what to say."

"I'm sure you must have given it *some* thought," I replied, sitting forward to rest my elbows on the table, "when you saw me sitting over here alone, enjoying my soup. Otherwise you wouldn't have come over."

She glanced at her brother-in-law who looked like he could bench press a ten-foot timber log without breaking a sweat. Surprisingly, he remained silent.

The sister shifted again. "I just wanted to tell you how sorry we are, and I want you to know that Jenn would never do anything like this if she didn't have that tumor on her brain. Really... it hit her like a giant tractor-trailer. A few months ago she was as normal as could be, the kindest, most generous, sensible woman I know. She's always been so helpful to me when *my* life's been a train wreck. If it weren't for her, I don't know where I'd be right now." Sylvie paused and looked down at her hands. "But that's beside the point. What I wanted you to know is that she's a good person who would never do something like this normally. And she's really sorry."

I inclined my head and leaned a little closer. "I thought she couldn't remember what happened. How can she be sorry?"

The husband, Jake, leaned forward as well. "She doesn't remember anything, but the cops have been questioning her relentlessly. She's handcuffed to the bedrail, for Christ's sake. Seriously, she's getting put through the wringer and I'm about to lose it."

Sylvie laid her hand on Jake's arm to try and calm him. "It's been rough on all of us. Jenn, especially. She woke up from the seizure with no memory of having it and was told she'd kidnapped a newborn. Believe me, she was shocked to hear that and she's trying very hard to remember. She wants to cooperate but she can't, and she's also dealing with the fact that she's having brain surgery tomorrow, and her husband just came back from Afghanistan, and he just found out she had a miscarriage and lost their baby..."

"Sylvie, stop," Jake said. "You're saying way too much."

"Why *are* you talking to me?" I asked with dismay.

They exchanged uneasy looks. Then Sylvie leaned forward. "Because Jenn wants to see you and talk to you before she goes in for her surgery tomorrow. We're hoping you'll come by and visit her."

"Visit her?" *Were they kidding me?*

But as I continued to stare across the table at the two of them, the fog of dismay in my mind began to lift. Miller had explained that the surgery would be high risk, so I could only assume that Jenn Nichols was seeking a way to atone.

I wish I could say I was moved by this plea, but when I thought of the emotional pain and grief my wife had endured the day before—and how I felt as if my guts were being ripped out of my body—my animosity stood like a brick wall.

"You want me to go to her room and *talk* to her?" I asked. "To the woman who abducted my newborn baby out of this hospital's nursery while my wife was recovering from a delivery that nearly killed her? Did you know she almost died in the OR? And do you have any idea how hard it was for me to tell her when she woke up that her baby was gone? That she'd been taken by a stranger and we had no idea where she was or if we'd ever get her back?"

Sylvie went pale. She wet her lips and stammered a reply as tears filled her eyes. "I know how it feels to lose a child, Mr.

James, and so does Jenn. We're both very, very sorry, and that's why she wants to see you. Please, will you visit her?"

I don't know why it happened in that moment, but something in me shook and trembled. Maybe it was because of the stricken look in Sylvie's eyes, or the fact that she said she knew what it felt like to lose a child. I wondered about those circumstances and realized I knew nothing about these people.

My attention shifted to the husband. He was staring at me with exasperated, bloodshot eyes. A muscle twitched at his jaw.

His wife had brain cancer.

He'd just found out she'd lost their baby while he was gone. Deployed. Fighting a war for all of us.

She might die tomorrow.

I swallowed over a sickening lump that rose up in my throat and found myself forming a careful reply. "I'll come," I said, "but Miller has to be there, too. I want him to hear everything so it's on the record. Will she be okay with that? Will *you*?"

Jake and Sylvie both nodded. "That sounds fair."

They gave me Jenn's room number and told me to stop by as soon as I could.

I don't know what I expected to see when I walked into Jenn Nichol's room twenty minutes later with Miller at my side. Since the moment I'd learned my baby had been abducted, I'd had a picture of the kidnapper in my mind. It was someone who embodied pure evil, a selfish monster who came to wield great power over the fate and happiness of my entire family, without a care for anyone she hurt. I'd felt completely at her mercy. Helpless and powerless, and I loathed this monster with every breath in my body.

But here she was before me—not a monster but a woman surrounded by her family. A woman in a hospital bed who was gravely ill with a brain tumor.

"Jenn," Sylvie said, rising quickly from her chair to take hold of my elbow and lead me toward the bed. "This is Riley James."

The woman regarded me with a mixture of unease and relief. Neither of us said a word while I took in the features of her face, no longer concealed behind an oxygen mask. She looked to be about thirty—younger than I imagined—and had long brown hair and melancholy eyes.

"Please sit down," she said, gesturing to the chair beside the bed. Miller stood at the foot of it.

"Will you all give us a moment?" Jenn said to her husband, sister and mother. At first they protested, then finally they gave in and filed out of the room.

Jenn reclined on the pillows, regarded me ruefully, and took a deep breath. "You must hate me."

Her greeting took me by surprise. "I can't lie," I admitted. "Yesterday I did, but today, I'm trying to work it out."

She looked down at her hands on her lap. "I can't blame you. I can't even imagine what you and your wife must have gone through when you found out someone took your child. It must have been terrible."

"It was."

She hesitated and kept her eyes downcast. "I don't know what Sylvie said to make you come here. I didn't think you would. You certainly don't owe me anything. So thank you for that." Her eyes lifted and met mine.

"I guess I was curious," I replied, wanting, for some reason, to offer an explanation.

She let out a small breath. "I can't blame you for that either, and I know there's nothing I can say to make up for what I did. I hardly remember any of it, but that doesn't matter. What they tell me is beyond comprehension—even to me—so I hope you'll believe me when I tell you how sorry I am. I honestly didn't know what I was doing."

I found myself sitting forward in my chair, resting my elbows on my knees, staring at her with a deeper, more intent curiosity. I studied her eyes and her cheeks and her mouth, every little nuance in her facial expression.

"You really don't remember anything?" I asked. Maybe I thought I could make her slip up and eventually confess that yes...she *did* in fact remember exactly what she had done, and that she had planned it all meticulously in advance. Every last detail.

I was glad Miller was there, watching and listening.

"Nothing at all," she replied, "up until the seizure. I do remember when it came on. I was in the restroom changing a diaper, and just before I collapsed, I felt confused and wondered whose baby it was on the table in front of me. I did my best to move her safely to the floor so that she wouldn't fall because I knew what was happening to me. I didn't want her to get hurt."

I found myself imagining the scene as she described it to me. "Thank you for that, at least," I replied.

"No, thank *you*," Jenn replied. "I was pretty out of it, but I vaguely remember, as I was coming out of it, hearing the sound of someone banging on the door and knowing that help was on the way, but I couldn't respond. I don't know how to explain it."

As I sat and listened to her describe other aspects of her seizure, I couldn't help but feel that she was telling me the truth—that she really had collapsed with no idea where she was or what was happening.

With that, came the first true inkling of compassion I felt. Maybe I felt it because she struck me as a reasonable, sane person with remorse, at least in that moment. There was nothing sinister about her, nor were there any veiled signs of darkness beneath the surface—something I was well acquainted with, having spent time in prison. I could spot evil in the eyes of a man at twenty paces.

Then it hit me like a brick that her sister had done the right thing to bring me here. Not just for Jenn's sake, but for my own.

Jenn glanced up at Miller who was standing against the wall. "See? Nothing new. Same story."

He smiled and slipped his notepad into his pocket.

Jenn returned her attention to me. "Thank you for seeing me and for finding me in that bathroom. I don't know what would have happened if help hadn't arrived when it did."

"You're welcome," I replied.

Tears filled her eyes as she reached for my hand. I found myself accepting hers in mine. "You're a good man, Riley James. You didn't deserve for this to happen to you." Then she smiled. "And your daughter's a very lucky girl to have a father who cares so much."

As I regarded the joyful, optimistic sparkle in Jenn Nichols's eyes, I felt surprisingly uplifted—as if great things were awaiting me just over the horizon. I had my newborn daughter back under my protection, and my beautiful wife was alive. Not only that... my wife loved me and believed in me, despite my many mistakes in this life. That was nothing new, I supposed. I'd been saying that for years. It's why I treasured her so deeply. It's why my life had been forever changed.

I sat in silence with Jenn Nichols for a moment, contemplating all of these things. Then I stood. "I should get back to my family."

Making my way to the door, I stopped when she said one more thing.

"Mr. James, will you also tell your wife how sorry I am? Please tell her it was the tumor. She certainly doesn't owe me her forgiveness. I don't expect it, but I need you both to know that I regret what happened. I wish I could take it back. I ruined what should have been one of the best days of your lives."

I faced her. "I'll tell her. And good luck tomorrow. I'll be praying for you."

Jenn sucked in a breath, like a gasp. Maybe she hadn't expected me to ever say a prayer for her. But how could I not? I was no angel myself. I'd committed my own sins, many of which I can't remember because I was drunk or high. I'd done things in my youth—destructive things—that I shudder to think of today. Was I now too arrogant to remember the life I'd once lived, the mistakes I'd made? Or to forgive others for theirs?

Jenn Nichols was no monster. She was just a victim of a cancer on her brain, through no fault of her own. It wasn't a choice she made. What mattered now was that I had my child back in my arms, and my wife, my angel, was alive, thanks to the doctors in this place. Or maybe all of that was thanks to a miracle or two, sent from heaven.

I felt sorry for Jenn Nichols. She was in police custody for a crime she'd unwittingly committed and on top of that, she was about to undergo brain surgery. She was not as blessed as I was today.

I knew, if anyone deserved my prayers, it was this woman before me—because she was still in great need of a few miracles of her own.

"Can I ask what you decided to name your baby?" Miller asked as we stepped onto the elevator. "Yesterday morning, you and Lois said you would know the right name when you saw her. Now you have."

I pressed the button to return to Lois's floor. "We decided to call her Leah."

Miller made a face. "Hmm. Funny."

"Why?" I asked.

"That's the second time I've heard that name today." He seemed to ponder the name while looking up at the lighted numbers counting down over the elevator doors. "Why did you choose it?"

I inclined my head inquisitively. "How about you tell me where else *you* heard the name? Then I'll tell you why we chose it."

We reached our floor and the doors slid open. "All right, then." Miller stepped off. "When I questioned Jenn Nichols about what she remembered from yesterday, all she could talk about was her seizure coming on, but she was able to describe a dream she'd had while she was lying on the floor in the restroom, before you tried to kick the door in."

"What was it?"

We walked past the nurse's station, heading toward Lois's room. "She said she dreamed there was a female doctor in the room taking care of her, telling her everything was going to be okay. The doctor picked up your baby and held her until we arrived." Miller's eyes met mine. "The doctor's name was Leah."

I stopped dead in my tracks. "You're kidding me."

Miller stopped as well. "No, that's what she said."

Feeling strangely euphoric and lightheaded, I began to back away from him.

"Where are you going?" Miller asked.

"I need to see Jenn Nichols again."

"Why?"

"I want to hear more about that dream." Still backing up, I quickened my pace.

Miller stepped forward. "Wait a second. You still haven't told me why you chose that name."

I turned around and walked quickly toward the elevators, tossing him a quick answer over my shoulder. "It was my sister's name."

My heart beat fast as I rounded the corner, pressed the button a few times and waited impatiently for a light to illuminate over one of the doors. Miller appeared beside me.

"Which sister?" he asked, just as an elevator arrived. "The one who died?"

"That's right." I stepped on, pressed button number five and gave him a smug, self-satisfied look. "And Jenn Nichols isn't a criminal," I added as the elevator doors slid closed between us. "She's a victim, Miller, and thank God someone realized she needed a little help from above."

Jenn
Post-Surgery

Thoughts came hazily into my mind as I regained consciousness in the hospital room. I felt confused for a few seconds, not sure where I was or what had happened to me, but at least I knew something was different. It wasn't like before. I hadn't suffered another seizure. Then I remembered saying good-bye to my husband and kissing him before they wheeled me off to surgery.

Now, there was a bandage wrapped around my head. I felt groggy. Maybe that's what made me realize I must have had the surgery—and I'd survived it.

"Baby, I'm here," Jake whispered softly, leaning over to kiss me on the cheek. "You did great. I'm so glad you're back." He pulled my hand to his lips and kissed the back of it numerous times. I felt his teardrop fall to my wrist and roll slowly down my arm to the inside of my elbow.

"Don't cry," I said in a trembling voice. "Everything's okay now."

He shuddered with a sob and kissed me on the lips. "I love you so much."

"I love you, too." I wanted to sit up and throw my arms around his neck, but that would have to wait. I needed to gain back some strength first.

He collected himself and sat back in the chair. "The doctor's on his way, but he told us the operation went like clockwork. He said they got the whole thing. But how are you feeling?"

"Okay," I replied, managing a small smile. "I feel smarter."

Jake laughed. "Your boss will be glad to hear it."

"Maybe he'll give me a promotion."

"As long as it comes with a decent pay raise." Jake kissed my hand again, then looked up when the doctor entered the room.

"You're awake," Dr. Phillips said. "Welcome back, Jenn. How are you feeling?"

"All right," I replied, though I wasn't ready to lift my head off the pillow yet.

"Good to hear." He listened to my heart with his stethoscope and nodded approvingly. "Can you tell me your name?"

"It's not written in my chart?" I asked teasingly. "And you said *I* was the one with memory problems. *Sheesh.*"

"Your sense of humor's intact," he said with a grin. "Name, please?"

"Jenn Nichols."

"Do you remember your birthday?"

"March 28, which makes me an Aries."

"Very good." He wrapped a blood pressure cuff around my arm, squeezed the ball a few times and took a reading. "BP looks good. Can you wiggle your fingers for me? Now your toes? Very good. And who's that person right there?" He pointed to Jake.

"That's my husband, Jake."

"Excellent." He wrote a few things down in my chart and moved around the foot of the bed. "Your head will be a bit sore for a while but we'll give you some pain medication to ease that. We'll be keeping you here for at least four or five days to make sure you're doing okay on all fronts, but so far everything looks terrific, Jenn. You were a superstar on the table. Seriously. Everything went perfectly."

"I like being a superstar," I replied. "Especially when I'm having brain surgery."

Dr. Phillips chuckled. "I suspect you'll be back on your feet in no time. Well done." He patted my foot under the sheet and left the room.

Jake squeezed my hand. "Sylvie and your mom should be here soon. They went home to shower a little while ago and I just sent them a text to let them know you're awake."

I took a deep breath and looked into his eyes. "I'm sorry for all this, Jake. I wanted everything to be smooth and easy."

"When is life ever smooth and easy?" he asked. "I'm just glad you made it through okay and we have the future to look forward to. I still feel like the luckiest man alive to be married to you, and no matter what happens from this day forward, we'll get through it, like we always have. I'm not worried."

I nodded in agreement and he kissed the inside of my wrist, drew small circles with his forefinger over the delicate blue veins.

"You know it's funny," I said. "When I invited Sylvie to live with me while you were gone, I thought I was going to be the one helping her out, but it turned out to be the opposite. I was the one who needed help, and she took good care of me, even when I was impossible."

"She's come a long way," Jake replied. "I think she's going to be okay. She seems stronger these days."

"I sure hope so."

"Not to change the subject..." Jake said as he bent down and reached for something in his backpack on the floor. "But I was thinking..."

Slowly he withdrew a newly framed photograph of the seaside cottage in Maine where we'd spent our honeymoon.

"You fixed it," I said.

"Actually, Sylvie did. And when I get back for good in the spring and you're feeling better," he said, "let's think about taking some time, driving out east and renting this house again. I checked and it's still available. We could take the sailboat out and maybe…if you're keen…we can try and make another baby."

Joy rose up within me. "That sounds like a dream, but don't forget I'm being charged for kidnapping."

"We're going to get you a really good lawyer, babe. We all know you weren't in your right mind. The doctors know it. Even Riley James knows it."

I swallowed hard over a lump in my throat and fought back tears. "But do you really want to have a baby with me, Jake? You're not just suggesting it for me?"

He laid a hand on my cheek. "Of course I want it. I might not have before, but clearly I was delusional because I've been so happy all this time, thinking about our future, as parents. I was dreaming about diapers and little league and helping with homework the whole time I was away."

His words were a soothing balm on my heart. "I'm so sorry I lost our baby," I said, "and for keeping that from you. I just didn't know how to tell you, and I was so confused all the time."

"It's not your fault," he replied. "You weren't yourself and I sure didn't make it easy for you, but you're better now. We'll try again."

I smiled as he climbed onto the bed and pulled me into his arms. "You know…" I said, running my finger over his chin, "I've always been an optimist and I've always believed that anything was possible, but now I believe it more than ever because of what happened to me. I don't want to waste any time. Life is so precious."

"We have to make every day count," Jake agreed. "We know that better than anyone, don't we?"

I nodded and together we gazed at the picture of the place where we'd spent our first days together as man and wife.

"Whenever I look at this," Jake said, "I feel happy, because it reminds me that I married the right woman. I'm glad I found you, Jenn, and that we're together, and somehow I know that we're blessed. We must be, because look what we just went through. And we're okay."

I rolled to face him and rested my head on his shoulder. "We're more than okay, Jake. And even though my head hurts and I might get charged for kidnapping, I swear I've never been happier in my life."

I touched my lips to his—to make sure he knew how much I meant it.

CHAPTER

Epilogue

Riley James

Sometimes I find it astounding when I look back on my life and remember the person I was in my youth—how angry and unhappy I was. I'm still not sure what caused everything to change. Was it just maturity, or was it life experience—the very worst kind that can knock sense into a man, like a wooden plank to the head?

Or maybe it was love. The day I met Lois was the day I truly began to see how far I could go, how high I could reach to become a better man. I was both bewildered and inspired by the admiration I saw in her eyes. All I wanted to do was live up to the greatness—and the goodness—she perceived in me. I never wanted to disappoint her.

We are that way with our children now, which is the opposite of how I was raised by my father. In his eyes, I was a failure at everything I tried and would never amount to anything. Unfortunately I believed him. Until I met Lois.

Together, as parents, we express our love to our children and admire their accomplishments with joy and enthusiasm, even the small ones like first steps and first words. Trudy is in second grade now, reading ahead of her level, and we make sure she knows how proud we both are. I never hold back when I tell her how amazing I think she is, and she responds with an ambitious spark in her eye like nothing I've ever seen.

I'm also proud to relate that Danny is a polite, well-behaved young man, interested in building things like his father. He has a passion for big machines like excavators and cranes. We're encouraging him to enjoy that, though it's anyone's guess what he'll want to be as he matures. He also loves airplanes and he's good at math, so when it comes to his dreams and what makes him happy, we're working to keep as many doors open as possible.

As for our baby, Leah, she's still learning what her thumbs can do, so the future is wide open for her.

I've had no dreams or spiritual encounters with my sister Leah since the day our baby was taken from the hospital nursery, but I can't help but believe she's out there somewhere, watching over all of us.

When I think of Jenn Nichols in that airport restroom dreaming of a doctor taking care of her, or when I recall how I tripped and fell that night, as if someone had stuck a foot out in front of me, how can I *not* believe? I confess, I never had much faith in Heaven before, but now I'm a true believer because clearly, there has to be some sort of magic in the universe when incredible things unfold as they do.

Every once in a while I think of my late sister with gratitude, and when I'm alone, I thank her out loud. I don't know if she can hear me, but I like to believe she can.

As far as Jenn Nichols is concerned, I'm pleased to report that the charges against her were eventually dropped. Miller—a decent man at heart—realized he had no case, at least not one that a prosecutor could win, especially since Lois and I were so sympathetic toward Jenn. We had no desire to see her convicted. Hadn't the poor woman been through enough?

If you're wondering if we sued the hospital—yes, we most certainly did and it was an easy win. They settled out of court and we have enough money now to put all three of our children through college and never worry about grocery bills again.

Nevertheless, I still work in construction because I find it satisfying…building things. When I come home at the end of the day, tired from a hard day's labor and needing a shower, I look around and know that I have everything I could ever dream of—a beautiful wife who loves me, three children I hold dearer to my heart than anything in this world, and a strength inside me that grew from struggles and lessons learned through terrible mistakes and the worst of hardships and regrets. But I pulled myself out of that pit. I survived it.

What can I say? I love my life. I've never been happier. Thank God I never gave up.

Questions for Discussion

⟨flourish⟩

1. Jenn describes herself as positive and optimistic, and she works hard to help her sister Sylvie adopt this attitude and improve her life. Discuss the relationship between the two sisters. How does it change from the beginning of the novel to the end? Also consider point of view and discuss how this plays into our perception of Sylvie and Jenn at different points in the novel.

2. Consider the theme of forgiveness in the novel in terms of each characters' experiences.

3. In chapter twenty-seven, after losing her baby, Jenn says this to Sylvie:

   "...I don't want him to think he has to carry me emotionally. He went through that before with his first wife..."

   ...I knew [depression] could happen to anyone. I just didn't believe it would ever happen to me. I'd always been incredibly rational and self-disciplined. I remained calm in a crisis when everyone else around me was in a panic—because I was in control of my mind and therefore my emotions. I almost never let them get the better of me.

   Discuss Jenn's thoughts here and what these statements say about her character at this point in the novel. Do you feel she is truly strong or—even without the brain tumor—do you believe she is in denial about how strong she is? If so, how and why?

4. From the moment we are introduced to Jenn in Chapter Eleven, who did you believe was responsible for the abduction of Riley and Lois's baby—Jenn or Sylvie? Or someone else entirely? Did your suspicions change as the story unfolded? If so, how and why?

5. Do you think, if Holly hadn't called Riley in the bar, that he would have taken the drink?

6. Compare the husbands of Lois and Jenn. How are they similar? In what ways are they different? What are the similarities that make them sympathetic characters in this novel?

7. In Chapters Forty-two and Forty-three, leading up to the moment Jenn has her seizure in the restroom, do you believe she thought the baby was her own?

8. Discuss how Jenn's and Sylvie's mother interacted with both daughters in terms of providing emotional support. What could she have done differently?

9. Do you believe in ghosts? Why or why not? Have you ever had an experience with a ghostly presence?

OTHER BOOKS IN THE
COLOR OF HEAVEN SERIES

The COLOR of HEAVEN

A deeply emotional tale about Sophie Duncan, a successful columnist whose world falls apart after her daughter's unexpected illness and her husband's shocking affair. When it seems nothing else could possibly go wrong, her car skids off an icy road and plunges into a frozen lake. There, in the cold dark depths of the water, a profound and extraordinary experience unlocks the surprising secrets from Sophie's past, and teaches her what it means to truly live...and love.

Full of surprising twists and turns and a near-death experience that will leave you breathless, this story is not to be missed.

"A gripping, emotional tale you'll want to read in one sitting."
　　　– *New York Times* bestselling author, Julia London
"Brilliantly poignant mainstream tale."
　　　– 4 ½ starred review, *Romantic Times*

The COLOR *of* DESTINY

Eighteen years ago a teenage pregnancy changed Kate Worthington's life forever. Faced with many difficult decisions, she chose to follow her heart and embrace an uncertain future with the father of her baby – her devoted first love.

At the same time, in another part of the world, sixteen-year-old Ryan Hamilton makes his own share of mistakes, but learns important lessons along the way. Twenty years later, Kate's and Ryan's paths cross in a way they could never expect, which makes them question the possibility of destiny. Even when all seems hopeless, could it be that everything happens for a reason, and we end up exactly where we are meant to be?

The COLOR of HOPE

Diana Moore has led a charmed life. She is the daughter of a wealthy senator and lives a glamorous city life, confident that her handsome live-in boyfriend Rick is about to propose. But everything is turned upside down when she learns of a mysterious woman who works nearby – a woman who is her identical mirror image.

Diana is compelled to discover the truth about this woman's identity, but the truth leads her down a path of secrets, betrayals, and shocking discoveries about her past. These discoveries follow her like a shadow.

Then she meets Dr. Jacob Peterson—a brilliant cardiac surgeon with an uncanny ability to heal those who are broken. With his help, Diana embarks upon a journey to restore her belief in the human spirit, and recover a sense of hope - that happiness, and love, may still be within reach for those willing to believe in second chances.

The COLOR *of* A DREAM

Nadia Carmichael has had a lifelong run of bad luck. It begins on the day she is born, when she is separated from her identical twin sister and put up for adoption. Twenty-seven years later, not long after she is finally reunited with her twin and is expecting her first child, Nadia falls victim to a mysterious virus and requires a heart transplant.

Now recovering from the surgery with a new heart, Nadia is haunted by a recurring dream that sets her on a path to discover the identity of her donor. Her efforts are thwarted, however, when the father of her baby returns to sue for custody of their child. It's not until Nadia learns of his estranged brother Jesse that she begins to explore the true nature of her dreams, and discover what her new heart truly needs and desires…

The COLOR *of* A MEMORY

Audrey Fitzgerald believed she was married to the perfect man - a heroic firefighter who saved lives, even beyond his own death. But a year later she meets a mysterious woman who has some unexplained connection to her husband....

Soon Audrey discovers that her husband was keeping secrets and she is compelled to dig into his past. Little does she know... this journey of self-discovery will lead her down a path to a new and different future - a future she never could have imagined.

The COLOR *of* LOVE

Carla Matthews is a single mother struggling to make ends meet and give her daughter Kaleigh a decent upbringing. When Kaleigh's absent father Seth—a famous alpine climber who never wanted to be tied down—begs for a second chance at fatherhood, Carla is hesitant because she doesn't want to pin her hopes on a man who is always seeking another mountain to scale. A man who was never willing to stay put in one place and raise a family.

But when Seth's plane goes missing after a crash landing in the harsh Canadian wilderness, Carla must wait for news...Is he dead or alive? Will the wreckage ever be found?

One year later, after having given up all hope, Carla receives a phone call that shocks her to her core. A man has been found, half-dead, floating on an iceberg in the North Atlantic, uttering her name. Is this Seth? And is it possible that he will come home to her and Kaleigh at last, and be the man she always dreamed he would be?

The COLOR of the SEASON

Boston cop, Josh Wallace, is having the worst day of his life. First, he's dumped by the woman he was about to propose to, then everything goes downhill from there when he is shot in the line of duty. While recovering in the hospital, he can't seem to forget the woman he wanted to marry, nor can he make sense of the vivid images that flashed before his eyes when he was wounded on the job. Soon, everything he once believed about his life begins to shift when he meets Leah James, an enigmatic resident doctor who somehow holds the key to both his past and his future...

Coming in 2015
THE COLOR OF TIME

Praise for Julianne MacLean's
Historical Romances

"MacLean's compelling writing turns this simple, classic love story into a richly emotional romance, and by combining engaging characters with a unique, vividly detailed setting, she has created an exceptional tale for readers who hunger for something a bit different in their historical romances."

—*BOOKLIST*

"You can always count on Julianne MacLean to deliver ravishing romance that will keep you turning pages until the wee hours of the morning."

—Teresa Medeiros

"Julianne MacLean's writing is smart, thrilling, and sizzles with sensuality."

—Elizabeth Hoyt

"Scottish romance at its finest, with characters to cheer for, a lush love story, and rousing adventure. I was captivated from the very first page. When it comes to exciting Highland romance, Julianne MacLean delivers."

—Laura Lee Guhrke

"She is just an all-around wonderful writer, and I look forward to reading everything she writes."

About the Author

Julianne MacLean is a *USA Today* bestselling author of many historical romances, including The Highlander Series with St. Martin's Press and her popular American Heiress Series with Avon/Harper Collins. She also writes contemporary mainstream fiction, and THE COLOR OF HEAVEN was a *USA Today* bestseller. She is a three-time RITA finalist, and has won numerous awards, including the Booksellers' Best Award, the Book Buyer's Best Award, and a Reviewers' Choice Award from Romantic Times for Best Regency Historical of 2005. She lives in Nova Scotia with her husband and daughter, and is a dedicated member of Romance Writers of Atlantic Canada. Please visit Julianne's website at www.juliannemaclean.com for more information and to subscribe to her mailing list to stay informed about upcoming releases.

OTHER BOOKS BY
JULIANNE MACLEAN

The American Heiress Series:
To Marry the Duke
An Affair Most Wicked
My Own Private Hero
Love According to Lily
Portrait of a Lover
Surrender to a Scoundrel

The Pembroke Palace Series:
In My Wildest Fantasies
The Mistress Diaries
When a Stranger Loves Me
Married By Midnight
A Kiss Before the Wedding - A Pembroke Palace Short Story
Seduced at Sunset

The Highlander Series:
The Rebel – A Highland Short Story
Captured by the Highlander
Claimed by the Highlander
Seduced by the Highlander
Return of the Highlander

The Royal Trilogy:
Be My Prince
Princess in Love
The Prince's Bride

Harlequin Historical Romances:
Prairie Bride
The Marshal and Mrs. O'Malley
Adam's Promise

Time Travel Romance
Taken by the Cowboy

Contemporary Fiction:
The Color of Heaven
The Color of Destiny
The Color of Hope
The Color of a Dream
The Color of a Memory
The Color of Love
The Color of the Season
The Color of Joy
The Color of Time

Made in the USA
Lexington, KY
04 November 2015